How to Not Fall for Your Ex, Book Four in the How to Not Fall series

Also by Meg Easton

Romancing the Spy romantic comedies

Spies Don't Fall for Their Asset

Spies Don't Fall for Their Rival

Spies Don't Fall for Their Neighbor (coming 2025)

Spiced Chais and Secret Spies

Holiday Lights & Cocoa Cookie Nights

————

How to Not Fall romantic comedies

How to Not Fall for the Guy Next Door

How to Not Fall for the Wrong Guy

How to Not Fall for Your Best Friend

How to Not Fall for Your Ex

————

A Mountain Springs Christmas

The Christmas Pact

The Christmas Bet

The Christmas Clause

————

Nestled Hollow Romance

Coming Home to the Top of Main Street

Second Chance on the Corner of Main Street

Christmas at the End of Main Street

More than Friends in the Middle of Main Street

Love Again at the Heart of Main Street

More than Enemies on the Bridge of Main Street

———

Love Started romances

It Started with a Sunset

It Started with a Note

It Started with a Glance

———

Silver Leaf Falls romance

Coming Home to Silver Leaf Falls

HOW TO NOT FALL for YOUR EX

HOW TO NOT FALL for YOUR EX

MEG EASTON

Contents

CHAPTER 1

Timini

I STRETCH after a good night's sleep.

Wait. Why am I so well-rested? And why is it so light outside? I fumble for my phone, knocking a bottle of lotion off my nightstand, and manage to light up the screen to see the time.

"No!" It's eight-oh-six, and I have a nine o'clock meeting with the director of an upcoming show at the Williams Theater in Hamilton Hall, and it's a good forty-minute drive to get there. I throw off my covers and leap out of bed. I can do this. I stand in the middle of my room, being pulled in a million directions at once until my head clears enough to think.

"Clothes," I say out loud, heading to my closet. Then I remember I already planned my interview outfit—a fabulous blouse and the perfect jeans. I even planned ahead enough to throw them into the washer. Then I got sucked into a Hallmark movie and hadn't remembered to put them in the dryer, so they're probably still damp, crumpled wads of fabric sitting in the washer.

I can find something else, no problem. I throw open my closet doors and look at what I have to work with. Which isn't much, because last night I had been feeling particularly proactive and I'd thrown most of what I own into the wash.

An oversized sweater with big, bold burnt umber and gold stripes calls to me, so I pull it out. I normally wear it with jeans, but every pair I own is currently residing with its friends in the bottom of the washing machine. Leggings with subtle geometric shapes are peeking out from one of my drawers, so I grab them. None of the colors on the leggings go with the sweater, but maybe I can pull one of the greens through to the top with a scarf. I scan the closet, and my eyes land on a vest whose green will work great.

I throw off my pajamas, swipe on deodorant, and pull on the outfit in about two seconds flat. It's not a pairing I would've ever picked under normal circumstances, but these aren't normal times. I glance in my full-length mirror. Surprisingly, it's actually an okay look. I grab a pair of light tan strappy wedges from my closet that can turn any outfit into something incredible and put them on. There. With these wedges and a confident stride, I can totally pull this outfit off.

As I race to the bathroom, I look at the time. Eight twelve. I brush my teeth (definitely not getting through the Happy Birthday song twice), then run a brush through my hair. At least I had the foresight to shower last night instead of this morning. It means that I have some hairs that bend at weird angles, though, so I just pull it into a messy bun.

After splashing water on my face, I put moisturizer on using both hands, then swipe on some mascara and force myself to slow down long enough to put lip gloss on without accidentally drawing a smile worthy of an emoji.

I race down the stairs and into the large dining area of the inn-turned-apartment where I live with my roommates. The bulk of my work is spread across the half-dozen round tables in the space meant for guests to eat breakfast. I grab my portfolio and the concept drawings I made for this particular play from a shelf along the back wall.

Then I start lifting piles of fabric and half-finished projects as I look for the pirate costume I'm so proud of designing and an eighteenth-century ball gown I just finished for a private school's sixth-grade play. It isn't adult-sized, but it's well made and I love it.

"I take it you're meeting with a client this morning?" my roommate, Addison, says as she cuts up a banana for her oatmeal in the kitchen end of the room.

"Potential client." I lift a stack of pattern pieces for a design I'm working on.

"Oh. Need help?"

I remember that I took the costumes upstairs to the closet in one of the extra bedrooms we have. "No, but I'll take one of those bananas to eat along the way." Addison tosses one across the room to me. I catch it and then race back up the stairs to grab the outfits.

Once I get everything shoved into my car and am on the road, the song on the radio ends, and a commercial plays that is probably for a gym or a life or relationship coach. Or maybe a pizza place. "If you don't figure out what you want in life, you'll never get it. So slow down and—"

I switch to a station with music. Whatever. No one has time for that. I take a bite of the banana and focus on getting to my destination.

My clients usually include directors for school plays—elementary through high school—and community theaters. My dream, though, is to have my own design studio and design the costumes for professional plays, just like the ones in the theaters at Hamilton Hall. If this interview goes well today, it could mean big things for my career.

By the time I drive through Gresham and pull onto Interstate 84 toward Portland, my heart rate has calmed, I take slow breaths and think only about the meeting I'm about to have. I will be pitching myself as the costumer to the director of the show *An American in Paris*.

Then a light on my dash catches my attention, and I glance down at my gas gauge. "No. No, no, no!" I've already driven a full day after the light came on. I forgot that I was going to wake up early and stop at the gas station before leaving Quicksand.

I wish my past self would quit having so much faith in my ability to get things done. Because there is definitely no time to stop and get gas now. The numbers on my dash say I will run out of gas in fourteen miles. I glance at the GPS on my phone that is leading me to Hamilton Hall—my destination is still fifteen miles away.

It's only a one-mile difference. All I have to do is a little more coasting than normal and not pull into a different lane and speed up to go around another driver. I pat the dash. "We can do this."

Twenty minutes later, I'm stopped at a red light. My fingers drum the steering wheel as I look at the dashboard that shows my range based on the gas in my tank is at zero miles. I murmur over and over, "Change to green, change to green." Finally, it does, and I press the gas slowly, trying to use as little of what fumes are still in the tank as possible.

I have just three blocks left to go when I pass a gas station. If only I had time to stop! But that is a problem for Future Timini. Present Timini is already late. Besides, two of the numbers in the gas price are ones, so that has to be a sign that I will make it.

A block from my destination, the gas—and my luck—runs dry. I hurriedly shift into neutral, flip on my right turn signal, and crank the suddenly hard-to-turn steering wheel to get my car off to the side of the road. It isn't the best parking spot, and it's still a block away from the building, but at least my car isn't blocking traffic at all.

But I am in a sixty-minute parking zone, so I pull a napkin from the stash in my glove box, a pen from my purse, and scrawl on the napkin, *Out of gas. Be back soon!* and then put it on my dash. Hopefully, that will be good enough. Then I get out, grab my portfolio with one hand and the two costumes with the other, and take off running toward the building.

My wedges hit the sidewalk with light clunks, in the graceless way wedges tend to do when running, the costumes swinging back and forth. I try not to think about what the bouncing motion is doing to my messy bun and whether it can still be called a bun at this point.

Halfway through the crosswalk, with the beautiful glass and brick building that shines in the sunlight just a hundred yards away, one of the straps on one of my shoes breaks free from where it connects to the sole, and my foot twists. Luckily, I catch myself and don't go down with my adorable shoe. I limp the rest of the way across the street. Not because my ankle is hurt, but because I can't walk normally and still cross the street while keeping the shoe on my foot.

Once I have made it to the sidewalk, I stop to check out the damage. Really, if I don't move, my shoe looks just fine. I test it a bit. It is the part by the toes that has broken free. If I kind of shuffle-walk, it will stay in place. Which is going to have to be good enough, because this is a really important meeting, and my wedges have a five-inch heel, so I can't exactly just take one of them off.

So I shuffle-walk my way right up to the front doors of the building and shuffle-walk my way to the receptionist. I take a quick glance at the clock on the wall behind her. Nine-eleven. Honestly, I'm impressed at how quickly I got here, all things considered. "Hello. My name is Timini Jensen, and I am here to meet with Aftyn Flint."

The receptionist opens her mouth to say something, but before she can get it out, a woman with a stern expression and an even sterner bun—the kind that doesn't have a single hair out of place—walks into the foyer. I immediately recognize her as the director. "You're late."

"I know," I say. "I am so sorry."

"Follow me," the woman says and starts walking down the hall.

Even with my additional five inches, courtesy of my struggling shoes, the woman still has me beat by a few inches. That isn't abnormal—at five-foot-one on a well-rested day, I am used to most people being taller than me. But those long legs of Ms. Flint's don't make it easy for me to keep up, especially when shuffle-walking. When the woman reaches the elevator and stops to see that I am still a dozen feet away, she glances at my footwear.

"I swear I know how to walk in these. The strap just broke as I was crossing the street and…" I trail off. I can tell that Aftyn Flint is not the type of woman who cares about excuses, so I speed up my shuffle-walk to something resembling a four-year-old pretending to be a choo-choo train and hurry into the elevator.

I finally take a breath in relief when we make it to the woman's office and I get to sit down. Ms. Flint stands behind her desk for a long moment, considering me, as if she is cataloging the strikes against me. Then she sits, and instead of easing in with small talk before heading into a conversational interview, the director says, "You've already wasted enough of my time, so let's just skip past the pleasantries. Pitch to me."

"Oh, um, okay." I pass my portfolio to Ms. Flint, but the woman doesn't even glance at it. She just keeps her steely eyes on me. So I talk. I tell about how a neighbor taught me to sew so I could help in her Etsy store when I was eleven, but shift to first talking about college, then to an amazing internship I had, and then to starting my own business, quickly shifting to the next item once it's apparent that each is irrelevant to the woman.

I've heard that giving some background helps the interviewer to see you as a real person, but I drop all background information pretty quickly and instead focus on telling what kinds of costumes I've made most recently.

As I am talking, the woman opens my portfolio and starts looking at the pictures of things I've made and my concept drawings for *An American in Paris*. She seems to be slightly more interested, so I stop talking and let her look. Maybe I should've just started with that.

It isn't long after, though, that the woman's eyes glance for the smallest second to the door. There is an invisible timer counting down to her exit through that door—I can feel it. So I grab one of the costumes I brought and unzip its bag while I talk as fast as I can.

"This is a pirate costume I designed." I pull the stylish costume out and hold it by its hanger. I start to give details about the piece but stop when Ms. Flint immediately stands and hurries around her desk to it. The woman fingers the details around the collar and then opens the jacket to better look at the poet's shirt underneath, inspecting the jacket lining and seams and buttons. This time, I know that silence is the best course of action.

"This is exquisite workmanship. What's in that bag?"

I unzip it and pull out the ball gown, holding it up. "I know that every director has their own spin they like to put on a play or show, and I incorporate whatever that is into the pieces that I design. For this one, the director wanted it to feel more modern and trendy, so I added the strong angular layers and the beadwork spray to help fit her vision."

"Stay here. I want to grab a colleague."

At least the woman seems impressed with my pieces. It probably won't undo the first impression she has formed of me, but it's something. Hopefully, it will be enough—I really want to be chosen to make the costumes for the show they are planning. Getting my costumes into a place like the Williams Theater could open so many more doors.

As I wait, I notice the stapler on the woman's desk. Oh, that is perfect! I grab it, open it up flat, and then maneuver myself and my leg so that I can get to the part of my shoe that has broken. I hold the strap against the sole of the wedge, then press the stapler against it and staple. With a whoosh of gratitude that it works, I put a second staple into it, just to make sure it holds tight.

And, of course, that's when Ms. Flint opens the door again. I hurry to right myself in the chair, bend the stapler into its original shape, and sneak it back onto the desk. The director narrows her eyes at me but then acts like she hasn't seen anything as she turns to her colleague.

"Naya, I'd like you to meet Timini Jensen. Timini, this is Naya Mallick."

The two of us shake hands, and then Ms. Flint goes to work showing Naya my costumes. Which is fine by me, because I really don't want to start my disastrous pitch over again. Both women ask me several questions, and then they both look at my portfolio.

"Thank you for meeting with me," Ms. Flint says. "We

will make a decision in a few days, and then we'll get in touch with you to let you know one way or another."

Well, based on how emotionless the director's parting words are, I'm not so sure I impressed them after all. I gather my things and head back to the elevator and then out to my car.

I put my portfolio and my sample pieces into the back seat then shut the door and sigh, wishing the meeting had gone better. Then I sigh at my car. I hate running out of gas. Not enough to have chosen to go to the gas station last night, apparently, but enough to not be happy with my decision not to. At least I keep an empty gas can in my trunk for situations like this.

There will be no hurrying to the station with my shoes in their current condition. As I trudge down the street, the gas can swinging in one hand, I'm grateful that I can at least trudge instead of shuffle-walk. Or worse, walk barefoot. Because at least this way, I still look fabulous.

But there is the cutest little girl ahead of me, maybe five years old, walking hand-in-hand with her dad. She has the same dark hair that I have, and it makes me wish I had grown up with a dad because the two of them are adorable.

And wow, that gas station is so much further away than I remember. About halfway there, one of the staples on my shoe pops loose, and I groan. I look up and down the street. I wish I were in a Hallmark movie right now. Wouldn't this be the perfect time for a meet-cute? A knight in shining armor would pull up to the curb next to me, his window down, his tanned arm resting across the door of his truck, and ask if I wanted a ride to the gas station. And I would say no, that I could do it myself, and then I'd keep walking.

Then my shoe would break the rest of the way, and I would turn to see that he's still there, a half-smile on his face, complete with an adorable dimple, and I would accept his help.

Instead, it is only me. No knight, no shining armor.

Although, with my next step, my shoe does break the rest of the way, so at least that part of the story comes true. I sigh and shuffle-walk like I'm a choo-choo train the rest of the way to the gas station.

CHAPTER 2

Jackson

MY EYES OPEN. It is still dark outside, but I can tell it is morning. About five seconds later, my alarm goes off, and I give myself a mental high-five as I turn it off. I always feel like I've just won a *Get Exactly the Right Amount of Sleep* award whenever that happens. It's probably just because my body is so used to waking up at six a.m. that it does it on its own, but I prefer to think it is because I'm disciplined enough to go to bed at the right time.

I stretch my arms wide before getting out of bed and dropping to the floor for fifty push-ups, just like I have every morning for the past eighteen years. When I was eleven, my favorite college basketball player came to speak at my school, and he said that he did fifty push-ups every single morning, first thing, no excuses. And then, anytime he needed to tackle a big project, or start a new habit, or get better at something, he could tell himself that he did that one thing consistently, so he could do anything consistently. He told us about what a difference it had made in his life.

It didn't hurt that the guy also had some seriously impressive arm muscles, and mine had been, well, the arm muscles of a sixth-grader who had grown two inches in the two months since school had started but hadn't gained a pound. So I decided right then that I was going to do the same. I no longer even have to think about it—it is just what I do.

After drinking a tall glass of water, brushing my teeth, and throwing on my gym clothes, I head down three floors to the gym for my section of apartments in this building. There are six treadmills, and three of them are filled by the same people who are with me every morning at six-fifteen—strangers I don't know outside of standing next to them in a row, running toward something none of us can see.

I give them each my customary nod and they give their customary nod back, a quick jerk for so little a motion, like they aren't willing to be pulled out of wherever they currently are in their mind. The woman always looks fierce and determined. She is probably running a marathon in her head. The older guy looks like he is imagining running on a sandy beach. The third one, though, usually looks like he is Rocky in that training montage where, at the end, he runs up the steps of the Philadelphia Museum of Art. Today, though, he looks more like he is running from zombies and they are about to win.

Me? I don't really picture myself running somewhere so much as I picture myself doing something other than running. That's why I never listen to music while I run. Sure, it is helpful to have the rhythm, but then it keeps the focus on the running, which makes forty-five minutes seem like hours. I run because it serves a purpose—to stay in shape. I don't run because I enjoy it.

I put in my earbuds, get on my treadmill, and go into my podcast app. All the daily business reports from the East Coast are posted by six. I find that if I turn the speed to double, not only can I get in all the ones I want to listen to in exactly forty-five minutes, but their fast, chipmunk-y voices are actually the perfect beat to run to. I get all my news listened to, and I have to focus to understand what they are saying at that speed, so it keeps my mind off the running and on their words.

Bam. Two birds, one stone.

When the last podcast sounds like it is getting close to wrapping up, I set the speed to a walk to cool down. At their final words, I stop the treadmill and go over to the weights. I spend fifteen minutes there, and for that, I *do* listen to music. Then I head back upstairs to shower.

At seven forty-two, exactly on schedule, I walk out of my room wearing slacks and a white button-down shirt. I use the remote to open the curtains covering my floor-to-ceiling windows along the wall of my living room and stand in front of them to look out over the Portland skyline from the twenty-first floor. I've been in this apartment for a year and a half now and never tire of the view.

I head to the kitchen, get out my bowl, spoon, cereal, and milk, and sit down at the bar to eat and watch cartoons. I'm not ashamed that cereal and cartoons are part of my morning routine. I decided long ago that it's important.

By eight-thirty, exactly, I've cleaned up breakfast, gone down to my car, driven the twelve minutes to Oliver Innovations—the business my family owns—parked, and made it up to the eighth floor. As I walk down the hall, I stop to poke my head into my sister Naomi's office. I know to not do anything more than wave hello. She has a fierce work ethic and swears that she gets more done between seven-thirty and eight-forty-five—before anyone is there to bug her— than most people get done by noon.

I pass right by my brother Ethan's office—Ethan doesn't believe any work worth doing should be done before ten, so it'll still be a while before he's in. Luckily, his job in sales seems to agree with his schedule. I do stop at the next door and say, "Good morning," to my sister, Emma, who's also Ethan's twin.

"Good morning!" she says, stopping organizing whatever papers are on her desk and coming over to give me a hug. She is the hugger of the family and would've seen it as a crime if I walked past her office without stopping for one.

"I've got a meeting at nine that I'm not ready for yet, but Dad wanted me to tell you that he needs to talk to you. I think he's in the break room."

I find both of my parents in the break room, along with one of my co-workers, Ramesh, all getting their morning coffee.

"Morning, sweetie," my mom says. "I've got an early stand-up meeting with my team in a few minutes, so I'll see you later." She gives my shoulder a squeeze as she passes me.

"Jackson!" my dad says. "Did you hear? Ethan got the

final retail chain we were hoping for in Delhi to agree to meet with you next week."

My eyebrows shoot up as a grin spreads across my face. I hadn't heard—it was probably something Ethan set up late last night. That is great news. My trip is going to be full of successes, I am sure of it.

"And Kim found another manufacturing possibility, so we've added that to your schedule, too. It looks like it'll be a full one."

"Just the way I like it."

Back when I decided to get my degree in International Business, I mostly had my family's business in mind. Or at least I hoped I would be able to use it there. I never imagined back then that all of my siblings and I would be working for Oliver Innovations, that we all would find our niches, or that I would love all the aspects of getting our products sold in international markets so much.

"And we should talk about some last-minute strategy," Ramesh says. "Do you have time in your schedule today to meet?"

I know my day is already packed, so I pull out my phone to check my schedule for any free windows of time. Ramesh steps up next to me to look. As soon as I unlock my screen, though, it goes straight to the classic *Phineas and Ferb* episode I ended on. I try to swipe it away quickly, but Ramesh has seen. Just because I'm not ashamed to watch cartoons with breakfast every morning doesn't mean I want my co-workers to know.

"Oh, hey! My kid loves that show, too!" Then Ramesh

gives me a look, probably remembering that I don't have kids so it was me who was watching.

I don't respond to Ramesh's comment like the man will simply forget if I forge on with enough force. "I've got twenty minutes at two fifteen."

"Two fifteen it is."

By the smile on Ramesh's face as he walks away, my forging on didn't make him forget.

Most of my day is spent lining everything up that I need to have in place before I leave for my trip on Friday. My trip requires coordination with sales and marketing, advertising, manufacturing, acquisitions, finance, and our law department, as well as more than two dozen contacts in India.

Since most of my day was spent in meetings, by the time six o'clock rolls around, I am a strange mix of exhausted and on fire, ready to start my trip right now. I loosen my tie and unbutton my top button. I'm organizing the papers on my desk that have been collecting on it all day when Ethan walks in and leans against my desk.

"You leave Friday morning, right?"

I nod.

"I'm going with Tricia to that business reception at the Burgesses on Thursday night. Want to double? I can set you up with Bronwyn. She's been asking about you."

"No."

"Are you not going at all?"

"I might go." I lean against the desk next to my brother. "I'm just kind of sick of dating people in our social circles. They're all…" I try to think about how to explain. "Like the people we went to school with when we moved my senior year, you know?"

"I think the words you're looking for are 'pretentious snobs.'"

"Actually, I'm kind of sick of dating people outside our social circles, too. I'll date a woman who seems great, and then suddenly everything will change, and I know she's Googled and found our family."

"It's like you can no longer tell if they like you for you, or if they like you for your income or status or job."

"Exactly."

"I get it," Ethan says. "So what are you going to do? Just not date anymore? Because bro, you're twenty-nine. Mom's only going to get on your back more and more about giving her grandkids."

"I know." I twist to look back at the pile of papers I haven't organized yet, trying to decide if I'm ready to make this decision. Because once I tell Ethan, I have to be ready. I take a breath. "You know Roman Powell, right?"

"Yeah. The CEO of LivenUP, right? I've met him a few times."

"A few weeks ago, we had lunch to catch up. He said that his company is coming out with a dating app, and they're doing a soft launch just in this area so they can see if there are any bugs before they release it nationwide. He asked me if I'd help him by trying it out, and I told him yes. The app opens for us today."

"A dating app? Really?"

I shrug. "It might be a way to meet someone who doesn't

know me. Everyone's bios only have first names, so they can't exactly Google me."

Ethan nods slowly. "True…so that might work. When are you going to do it?"

I walk around to the other side of my desk and start arranging my papers. "I was thinking of creating a profile tonight."

"Tonight?" Ethan stands up from my desk and turns to face me. "Dude, in two days, you are leaving the country for three weeks. Do you really think now is the best time?"

A smile spreads across my face. "It's exactly the best time. Hopefully, I'll find a few women who are interesting. We won't be able to meet in person because I'm out of town, so we'll get plenty of chances to talk and get to know each other before they find out who I am."

"Huh. Sometimes I don't give you nearly enough credit for being brilliant."

I laugh. "So does this mean you want to try it with me?"

"Nope." Ethan shakes his head. "I like dating pretentious snobs and gold diggers. I figure it'll keep Mom from coming to me for grandkids for a little longer. I mean, I am the younger twin, and I'm nearly three years younger than you, but it doesn't hurt to have redundancies in place."

"You keep your redundancies," I say as I file the papers and turn off my laptop. "I'm going to find someone I want to go on more than one date with."

"Just promise me one thing," Ethan says as we walk out of the room.

I turn off the light and pull the door closed behind me. "What's that?"

"Don't...overthink it. Just have fun. Don't make any charts or plan things out in detail."

I'm not going to promise my brother anything, but I sure will try.

CHAPTER 3

Timini

MY MORNING MIGHT NOT HAVE BEEN optimal, but at least it waited to start raining until I was on my drive home. And something about the drive home makes the solution for the Cheshire cat costume I need to make suddenly pop into my head. By the time I get home, my mind is flooded with ideas that need to be sketched, planned, and created.

My roommate, Peyton, is a personal chef and often cooks for her clients in the kitchen at the other end of the dining room from where I work. Peyton is at the home of a client today, though, so I have the entire room to myself.

The more I work, the more the project comes together. I start with sketching, but before I have even sketched out the full thing, I'm sketching close-ups of different parts and scribbling notes into the margins. I never manage to get a project fully sketched before it calls me to start working with paper and fabric on a dress form.

For the more difficult parts, I start with cheap muslin before using the actual fabric, and for some parts, I just throw caution to the wind and start with the fabric for the finished product. As I work, more and more details come to mind to make it even more fabulous.

I hear the front door open and voices chatting. Then, Bex and Roman walk into the kitchen and Roman says, "Cool costume. Is this for *Alice in Wonderland?*"

I look at him in confusion. "Why are you home so early?"

"It's after six."

What? It can't be. I glance at the clock on the wall. Just in case I'm inclined to not believe it, my stomach growls loudly just to prove that so much time has passed since I ate that banana. I stand and stretch my muscles that have been sitting, crouching, and standing in way too many places in this room for way too long.

"Remember that dating app you suggested my company make?" Roman says.

I look over at him. "It's finished?"

Roman nods, looking like a proud parent. "It went live for beta testers in this area today. Once we get any kinks worked out that we find by having real people use it, we'll release it nationally. Are you willing to be one of our testers?"

I like to date, but just like my mom and my sister, I'm usually better off when I'm not dating anyone. So even though I like it, I don't always take the time to do it. And when I do, I am terrible at it. Ridiculously terrible.

Actually, I'm really good at finding guys who are pretty —on the outside. It's the pretty on-the-inside guys that I am terrible at finding. There must be some kind of look about a guy that I'm drawn to that just also happens to make for a not-great dating experience. The guys always tend to be not bright, not nice, or not a good fit.

Which was why I'd suggested to Roman that his company make a dating app that doesn't show people's pictures. That way, people like me won't make bad choices based on what their options look like—they would get to know them first.

It sounded like a great idea at the time. Obviously, it had to Roman, too, or he wouldn't have had his company invest months into developing and testing the app. As perfect as it is in concept, now that it's actually here, I am a little afraid that I'll mess things up completely if I don't have anything to go on when choosing guys.

"So, what do you say?" Bex asks. "Roman was showing it to me—it has some pretty cool features."

"I don't know. I'm not sure I want to date right now." Life is going pretty good lately. Well, okay, maybe not good, *exactly*. But it's going well enough. Do I want to mess it up by dating?

Peyton and Addison must have gotten home from clients' houses, because they both walk into the kitchen, laughing about the awkwardness of using the restroom at a client's home and realizing the toilet paper is out.

Bex turns to them. "I need your help talking Timini into using Roman's dating app."

"You don't want to use it?" Peyton asks. "But you were the one who suggested the app in the first place."

"I know. It's just…" How can I even explain? They've all

found guys who are perfect for them. And with each of my roommate couples, they are better together than they are separate. But that isn't the way it is for me. Once upon a time, Bex was in my corner about this. Now, I'm the only one in an inn full of love who is walking around loveless and not unhappy about it.

"I've always been bad at choosing who to date. I thought that not seeing their pictures might make it better, but who says that's actually what my problem is? What if I'm just bad at interpreting the facts I have, and I'll be even worse at it when there's less information to go on?"

"I think we did a good job of giving you more to go on," Roman says. "Can I show it to you and then you decide?"

Of course, I am going to say yes to that. Roman took my suggestion to create the app, after all. I am excited to see what it's all about, even if I never use it. I unlock my phone and hand it to Roman. His finger flies over it for a moment, and then he hands it back to me, the icon with two text bubbles—each with a heart—showing on my screen. I tap on it, and then put in my name.

"Why is it asking to take my picture? I thought this was a picture-free dating app."

"That's so no one will hack your account," Roman says. "It'll compare it to your face each time you log in. It'll ask for your driver's license, too. We want to make sure we keep all hackers, catfishers, and creepers away. The guys you'll see in the app will only be verified accounts."

"Nice." I snap a picture of myself, then glance at the table currently covered in fabric scraps where I'm fairly certain I sat down my purse earlier. I go over and start digging through it, but it isn't there. Halfway through checking under all the fabric detritus at half of the other round tables, I remember that I left it on a half-height bookshelf I use for folded fabric.

After putting in all the required information to get an account, it brings me to a screen to create my profile. Then I look at Roman. "It's all yours. Sell me on it."

"Okay," Roman says, and it is clear by the way his face lights up that he is proud of this app. "Your profile has four parts: your bio, your personality traits, personality traits you're looking for, and how serious a relationship you want."

I nod. That sounds like good info.

"The bio is pretty standard. This is the relationship scale. You can slide it all the way to the left if you are just looking for friendship or all the way to the right if you're looking for marriage. Or anywhere in between. That way, you can find someone who is looking for the same thing in a relationship that you are."

That's good. If I decide to do this, I can just choose an option that shows I don't want anything too serious.

"For personality traits, you can just tap on the buttons on the screen that fit you. Then you tap the ones you're looking for in a match. Later, when you are flipping through the guys in the app to find potential matches, little icons will show at the top if they match what you're looking for."

Okay, that is actually pretty cool. Maybe with that, I can make better choices on whom to even start chatting with.

"There are a lot of safety features built-in. Other people on the app will only ever see your first name, and they won't have any of your contact information. So if you only communicate through the app and then decide you aren't really a good match with someone, you can un-match them and they won't have any way to contact you.

"And if you do like them and decide you want to meet in person but are a little nervous about that, just click right there on the 'Track My Date' button. It'll turn on GPS tracking and let you put in the number of a friend. If you go somewhere unplanned or if you are out longer than expected, it'll notify the friend to check on you. If they can't get in touch with you, they'll have a link they can press that will notify the police and give them your date's contact info. It'll keep you and your date safe, even if you don't have each other's contact information."

I hadn't realized that was an obstacle to my wanting to use the app. Maybe this app *is* just what I need to find some-one. It doesn't mean I'm not still hesitant, though. I look into the faces of my roommates. "I don't know. Do I even want to date someone right now?"

Addison shrugs. "You're always saying that you can't get serious with a guy because you always seem to choose those who aren't your type on the inside. Maybe this will help you to find someone more serious."

"But do I want to find someone more serious?" Sometimes I like living in a fantasy world and totally do want what my roommates have. Other times, I am a realist and don't want to even try. When I was growing up, my sister and I learned to dread hearing our mom say the words, "Things are getting serious with the man I'm dating," because it never turned out well.

"You don't have to find someone to be in a serious rela-tionship with," Bex says. "How about just finding someone for group date nights?"

"Ooh. That sounds good. I like group dates." It doesn't have to go beyond that at all. No long-term relationship needed. "Okay, but if I do this" —I meet each of my room-mates' eyes— "you have to promise not to push things between me and anyone I date to be more serious. Even though you're all head-over-heels in love and want the same for me. I'm just looking for someone for date nights with you all. Deal?"

Peyton squeals and gives me a hug. "I promise. We all do. Right?"

They all nod. They seem like they'd agree with anything to get me to try the app, so I add, "And I should get crème brûlée since I'm the only one who has stuck to our 'No falling in love' pact."

Bex laughs loudly. "Girl, you've earned it."

I sit at the dining table and they all gather around to help me make my dating profile, and I bring up the first thing. "Ugh. The bio." That's always the hardest part. "What kinds of things should I even put on this?"

"Say that you're a burst of energy in a little tiny pack-age." Bex makes her hands into fists and then opens them wide, fingers splayed. "Like a firecracker."

"Or an energy drink," Addison says.

Peyton sits down next to me. "Say that you're beautiful and sassy and will never get mad at him for being late."

I laugh. "Only if he never got mad at me for the same."

"I know," Addison says. "Put that you are spilling over with talent and creativity."

"Oh," Peyton says, sitting up straighter. "Maybe you could have quotes from us. You know, like some guys put *'Such a sweet boy'—my grandma* in theirs. We could tout all your good qualities."

I shake my head. I do not like where this is going at all.

"Guys don't want to read a list of everything awesome about a woman," Roman says. "They want to discover that as they get to know you. On a dating profile, they just want you to be real. Genuine. Someone they feel they could relate to."

"Thank you," I say. It's helpful to get some advice from my target audience. I tap my finger against my lips. What is most real and genuine about me? "Hmm. Okay, so how do I say that I'm a hot mess without actually using those words? Authenticity is one thing. Scaring them away is another."

Roman just chuckles and shakes his head.

"Well," Bex says, "you focus on the thing that needs the most immediate attention. Maybe something with that."

"True. *That* I am good at. Okay." I type part of it into my phone.

"Don't forget to put what your job is," Addison says. "I think that tells a lot about a person in just a few words."

I nod and type that in.

"Hobbies, too," Addison says.

Hobbies… Do I have hobbies? Creating wearable masterpieces has been my hobby practically my whole life, and then it became my career. I don't think I can still count it as a hobby, even though it still feels like it. "Do impromptu dance parties count as a hobby? Because I'm a fan. And I really don't want to say something like 'I collect buttons,' or 'When most people people-watch, I outfit-watch,' because then he'll think I'll be judging his."

"Which you totally will," Bex says, "since you notice what people are wearing more than most."

I point a finger at Bex. "But I don't judge. I just study them, because they tell so much about the person."

"What about your love of high heels?" Peyton asks. "Then it gets the fashion thing in there without making it sound like you'll be judgy."

"Oh, good one." I type more into the app. "Okay, tell me how this sounds. 'Costume designer by day, cookie connoisseur by night. Hater of to-do lists. Skilled at putting out the nearest fire. Lover of high heels and the number one.'"

"That's really good," Addison says. "Now add a part about what you're looking for in a guy."

"But I don't know what I'm looking for in a guy. Besides 'pretty on the inside.' But I don't think I can put that."

Bex shakes her head. "Girl, you need to spend some time figuring that out. You can't find what you want if you don't know what you're looking for."

Yeah, I probably should. Maybe that is why my dating life has never gone anywhere. "No, do you know what? I've got this." I read it out loud as I type it in. "Looking for a guy who doesn't judge a girl by her inability to cook food that shouldn't be blackened, can reach objects on high shelves, and can handle going on group dates with my roommates who are all ridiculously in love."

"I love it!" Peyton says. "Now just add a call to action."

When my eyebrows draw together, Peyton explains. "If you give them something to chat with you about, they'll be more likely to start up a conversation."

"Ahh. Gotcha." Peyton did seem to find a lot of dates very quickly when she was trying to fit fifteen dates into a single week, so she knows what she's talking about. I bite my lip as I type things in, backspace, try again, delete it all, try again, and then fix the errors.

"Like this? 'Need a taco recommendation? As a starving artist, I can suggest the tastiest and most inexpensive tacos in Portland and all surrounding cities. Or, tell me your favorite place to get a taco, and I'll rate it like I'm a food critic.'"

"Yes!" Peyton says, clapping.

"Okay, now I pick twelve of my traits." Luckily, the list seems to have mostly positive traits so I don't have to feel guilty about not choosing the negative ones I have but would rather not mention. I scroll through quickly, tapping any that sound like me. Active, adventurous, curious, daring, determined, empathetic, flexible, free-thinking, imaginative, observant, and playful. I count, and when I get to eleven, I tap on sentimental for the twelfth.

"And five traits I would like in a man. That list is long! How do I choose?"

"Well," Addison says, "there will probably be some traits you'll want in a man that matches yours. But the best kind of partnerships are ones where you balance each other's strengths and weaknesses. So pick some that would balance you."

"Okay…" I scan the list. "Then I definitely need to add Clean, Focused, and Organized, since I am none of those.

Hmm. And I think I'm going to choose Adventurous and Flexible or I don't think things would work out so well with us."

Which leaves me with one thing: the sliding scale of how serious I want to be. I move the little indicator from left to right along the options, reading each one.

Seeking friends
Down for coffee
Keeping it casual
Looking for romance
Seeking something serious
Ready for a ring

I select *Keeping it casual*. Once I tap *Submit*, a message comes up on the screen that reads, *Success! Your profile will be approved within the next twenty-four hours, then get ready to start matching!*

I look up at Roman. "I have to wait twenty-four hours to actually use this?"

He shrugs. "It's the price of having verified accounts."

When I decide to do something, I want to do it now. None of this waiting-for-twenty-four-hours business. I need to find something else to do for the next twenty-four hours to get my mind off it, or I'm going to go crazy.

CHAPTER 4

Jackson

I'VE JUST PARKED in my reserved spot in the parking garage for my building and am heading to the lobby when my little sister, Emma, calls.

"Are you home?"

"In the building."

"Great. I'm coming over to help you with your dating profile."

"Wait!" I head toward the mailboxes, where several other residents are picking up theirs, too. "Don't come. I'm having second thoughts."

"Not allowed. You already made this decision."

"Is now really the time, though? I'm leaving in a day and a half, and I'm going to be gone for three weeks." Sure, I just told Ethan that leaving for three weeks makes it the perfect time. And I still believe that—if I'm going to do it at all. But it feels like a good stalling tactic as far as Emma is concerned.

"That's not the reason you're stalling."

I curse under my breath. Emma and Ethan have the whole *I'm your twin so I can read your mind* thing going on. But I swear that Emma can use it on everyone, not just Ethan. Or at least everyone in our family. It makes it hard to do things like lie about the true reason I'm getting cold feet in regards to a dating app.

I put my key into my box, open it, and pull out the half a dozen envelopes inside. "It sounded like a good idea when I was talking with Roman about it. I was even on board earlier today. But, I don't know. Now I'm not so sure."

"Why." It is not a question—it is a demand. For most of my life, I have fought Emma on her demands. She is the youngest and I am the oldest, so if anyone is the boss of anyone, she isn't the boss of me. But she is relentless on some things, and it sounds like this is one of them. It is always easier and faster to give in. Sometimes easier and faster wins, and sometimes it doesn't. Today, I need to get to my apartment and get some last-minute things done before my trip.

I heave out a long breath and head toward the cleaners at the back of the lobby so I can pick up my shirts. "Because it feels like admitting defeat."

"Explain."

"Dating apps are for people who can't get dates on their own." I'm not about to admit that not being able to get dates on my own means I have lost the ability. I'm kind of worried that maybe I have, but I'm nowhere close to being ready to full-on admit it.

"No," Emma says, dragging out the word, "they're for

people who aren't meeting people to date in their normal routines. You aren't meeting the types of people you want to date doing what you're doing, so you need to do something different."

"Maybe." The types of people I do meet are very much not the type I want to be in a relationship with. "But it's also a lot of work setting everything up, chatting with a ton of people to narrow it down to who I should date, and going on lots of dates to find someone with relationship potential."

"And you're afraid that if you fail using a method of finding dates that you already see as second-class, it'll make you feel like a loser."

"What? No, I'm not afraid."

"Then do it."

She is goading me. Earlier, it was worth it to give in to her need to be the boss. Now it isn't. "Not going to happen."

"You'd rather die alone, after a life spent in unfulfilling relationships."

Of course, I wouldn't. "Sounds good. Sign me up for the unfulfilling life."

"You are impossible."

"Hang on." I lower the phone and hand my ticket to the clerk behind the counter, an older man who runs the kiosk with his wife. As the man shuffles off to find my shirts, I turn to lean against the counter. I am just lifting the phone back to my ear when a mom holding the hand of a little boy, probably about three years old, walks toward the kiosk.

When they are within a dozen feet, the little boy holds his arm out, his finger pointing at me. "Look, Momma!"

The boy's mom pushes his hand down and says, "Sweetie, we don't point at people, remember?"

The little boy puts his arm out again, but this time, his hand is in a fist. "Momma, look. See the direction that my arm is pointing? Is that my daddy?"

The woman's face immediately goes red. She pushes her son's arm down again, opens her mouth like she is going to say something to her son, but then gives up and just looks at me. She puts her fingers on her forehead, possibly because she is trying to see how hot her face has gotten in a span of five seconds, or possibly because she is trying to hide her face. "I'm so sorry. It's just your suit. His dad wears one to work, so he was really just asking if you and his dad work at the same place. You know—if you're the same as his dad."

I can't keep the smile off my face. "It's fine."

She glances back at her son, and then puts her hand back on one side of her face, covering one cheek and eye as she looks back at me. "I swear he knows who his dad is but he still says that to everyone. And, um" —she glances toward the elevators— "we're just going to go now. Bye."

I'm still grinning as I put the phone back to my ear. "I'm ordering Thai food. Be here in twenty minutes if you want to eat while it's warm."

"You're going to do the dating app?" Emma's excitement is so loud that I probably didn't even need to lift the phone to my ear.

"I am." I want my own little kid who is going to embarrass me in public, and the only way I'm going to get that is if I meet someone worth marrying. And this app sounds like a possible way to do that.

"Then I'm going to run—okay, jog—and be there in ten."

Fifteen minutes later, I'm sitting on the couch in my apartment, staring at my phone. So far, all I've managed to do after ordering the food is enter my name and take a picture of myself and my driver's license. The rest is intimidating.

My front door opens and my sister walks in. "Okay, I know I'm later than I said, but it had started to rain, and running while holding an umbrella is weird. But I did meet the delivery guy in the lobby with the food. He said you already paid but had me sign your credit card receipt. I decided that you're feeling generous today, so I tipped him fifty bucks for you."

I shake my head, chuckling. I have no doubt she did.

Once we get out the food and I have a few bites of yellow curry and rice in me, I pick up the phone again, as if inspiration has struck while it has been sitting on my coffee table.

It hasn't. The bio is still as blank as before.

Emma takes a big bite of stir-fried rice noodles. Before she even finishes chewing, she says, "You know..." She swallows. "You don't have to tell your life story. You just have to give a little something that will make someone want to know more."

No pressure. Piece of cake.

She sets her box of Pad Thai on the coffee table. "You don't want to attract the same type of women that we see at all the functions we go to, right? So let's start with what you don't want women on the app to know."

That part is easy. "My last name, who I work for, probably my job title."

She nods. "That's easy enough. The app won't even show your last name. Okay, so what's something you do want them to know?"

That's the hard part. Everything I think of sounds too dumb to utter, let alone type.

After a moment of me staring at the screen again, Emma says, "Okay, type this: *The first thing people notice about me:* and then press enter."

I do. I wait for her to tell me what to type next, but by her exasperated huff, I guess I'm supposed to come up with that. Okay, so something about my looks. Women I've dated in the past have told me a few things they liked about my looks, but I'm pretty sure they were just telling me what they thought I wanted to hear. Nothing about them, though, was genuine, so I doubt any of those things were, either. So I try to think of what I've heard from complete strangers. "I've been told I have nice ears."

She raises an eyebrow. I figure it might be enough for her to take pity on me and tell me what to put. But then she just shrugs. "You know what? Put it."

"For real?"

"Sure. It's different. A little intriguing. Besides, I know I judge a guy based on how cute his ears are."

I grab a couch cushion and toss it at her.

She picks up her noodles again. "Now write *Three things I can't live without,* and then come up with three things."

Okay, things. This shouldn't be too hard. I run through a typical day in my mind, thinking about what things are important to me and weeding through anything that hints at my family having money or me having a very well-paying job.

Things like the view from my apartment (my day definitely goes better when I take the time to admire and appreciate it before heading to work).

Or my favorite restaurant (which serves a Japanese Wagyu ribeye that makes me think that is exactly the food they are going to be serving in heaven, but which also costs roughly the same amount as a month of my entire food budget in college).

Or my office chair that is so perfect I could sit in it all day long if needed, and my back wouldn't even hint at being upset about it. (Yeah, that one cost more than the car I drove all through college.)

Or anything about my car.

I do include in my bio one extravagance, though. *The cleaner who irons my shirts so I don't have to.* I ironed my own dress shirts from the time my mom started making me iron my church shirt when I was eight until the end of my first year working at my current position at Oliver Innovations, and I've always hated it. The moment I was making enough to have someone else do it, I celebrated.

Then I type *The day planner in my phone*. Emma is waiting patiently, but her eyes never leave me as she eats bite after bite, so I force myself to think just so she will eventually stop staring. I add *Cold cereal and morning cartoons*. I don't have to put the reason. People who see it will probably assume I'm a kid at heart, or nostalgic, or that I'm lazy. I don't care if they think any of those things. I haven't ever told anyone the real reason, but it is definitely on my personal *Things I can't live without* list.

The moment I finish, she says, "Okay, now put *What I love the most.*"

"Easy. Family." As Emma throws her hands over her heart in an exaggerated motion of being touched, I say as I pretend to type, "Well, not all of them equally," and she throws the pillow right back at me.

"Okay, now put…" She looks up, thinking. "I don't know. Something like *Extras* or *More about me.*" When I do, she says, "Now list stuff like your job. I mean, obviously, you don't want to put 'I'm the VP of International Business.' Just give a clue. Say you work in business or that you travel a lot for work."

I nod and start typing.

"And say what you like to do in your spare time."

Honestly, I work in my spare time. If it's not at work, it's at one of my family's charities. Whatever look I have on my face must tell Emma I'm going to struggle. "Just say what you most like to do when you go out with friends or go on dates. It'll help women know what kinds of dates you'll likely want to go on."

Okay, that makes it a little easier.

"And you can say that you enjoy helping kids learn to read without mentioning our family's charities."

"True. Okay, I will."

"Now lighten it up a bit. Tell something random and inconsequential."

There is no way I could have ever done this on my own. How does Emma even know what my bio needs? If I had done this myself, it would have been organized, thorough, and probably would have put anyone to sleep who made it all the way to the end. I add *I can shower in seven minutes flat.*

I look at Emma. She reads over my shoulder, nods, and then says, "Now just give them something that'll make an initial conversation with you easy. Give them something to talk to you about."

Nothing comes to mind. Emma breathes that exasperated breath she perfected years ago and says, "Write 'If you like movies, cheese, or traveling, we should chat. If you like all three, we should definitely meet in person at some point.'"

That is good. Once I type it in, I say, "Okay, now it wants me to pick twelve personality traits."

"Hand it over." Emma holds her hand out to me, palm up.

I pause, trying to decide if that's a good idea. She holds her hand out a little more insistently, so I put it in her palm.

"Just so you know, I'm choosing your twelve *and* the five for her."

When she hands it back, I glance through the list she's chosen. *Active, adventurous, appreciative, ambitious, clean, confident, decisive, disciplined, focused, innovative, leader, organized.* All right. That isn't too bad. At least she didn't put embarrassing things on the list like I thought she was going to.

"Obviously," she says as I look at the list, "'confident' is based on everything except writing your own bio for a dating app."

"Obviously. Now defend your choices for what I'm looking for in a woman." I actually think that it's a pretty great list, too, but I have to give my sister a hard time.

"Okay, adventurous and active, because you'll want to do things together that you both enjoy. Playful, because you need to get out of your shell and your routine more often. Flexible, because she'd need to be to balance your rigidity." She shoots me a look. "And focused, because it fits with who you are. Down-to-earth wasn't one of them, so you'll just have to keep an eye out for that one on your own. Now don't question my choices—just move onto the seriousness slider."

I read through the list. Honestly, I want to choose *Ready for a ring*, but I don't want to scare anyone. So instead, I choose *Seeking something serious*.

"Should I press Submit?"

"Yes!" she shouts. "Submit!" Like she's afraid if I don't press it in the next one-point-two seconds, I will delete the app instead. Her excitement makes me stop for a moment just to question if that might be the best option.

Instead of letting my mind go in that direction, though, I think of the little kid downstairs and how much I want my own someday. I tap *Submit* with conviction. When the message comes up saying that my profile will be approved within twenty-four hours, I am relieved. I don't want Emma looking over my shoulder as I scroll through potential matches.

CHAPTER 5
Timini

I AM WORKING on designing a Revolutionary War-era costume that comes to me in the shower. It isn't even for a job—it's just an idea that is too amazing not to start right now. I am a little (okay, a lot) focused on it when my phone starts blaring my ringtone.

"Timini!" Peyton says from behind the kitchen island where she is making something that smells divine. "That about gave me a heart attack!"

"Sorry!" I have to have it loud, though, if I want any chance of finding it when it rings. The song I use as my ringtone keeps playing at full volume as I go from table to table to find the one that holds the phone, then search under each layer to find it.

"Hello?" I say as I answer, out of breath from my frantic search and worry that I haven't caught it in time.

"Timini Jensen?"

"This is her."

"Hello, this is Aftyn Flint."

My mind is so deep in what I am working on that it takes me about a second and a half to recognize the name as the woman I interviewed with yesterday. Then I listen in disbelief and shock as Ms. Flint tells me that they were so impressed with my work that they decided they want to use me for two separate projects, and she gives a little information about what the scope of each will be.

When she says she'd like me to come in to discuss everything further and to make it official, I can barely find my voice enough to agree to the date and time.

I hang up the phone and drop into a chair at the dining table, stunned.

"Is this good news or bad news?" Peyton asks.

"The best," I say as what has just happened starts to sink in. "I get to design costumes for *An American in Paris*, so lots of period clothing, and another director isn't happy with the Prince Charming costume their costumer made for *Cinderella*, so they want me to do that, too. Costumes for two shows, and both are at Hamilton Hall! I know that one of them is in the Williams Theater. I don't know about the other. *Hamilton Hall!*"

Peyton doesn't know a ton about my industry, but she gets excited for me anyway and comes around the kitchen counter to hug me and squeal and congratulate me.

I want my own design shop. And not just someday, like when I'm fifty, but soon. Like by the time I turn thirty. That is only two years away, and I have felt like the path I need to take to reach my goal is by first designing for a show at

Hamilton Hall. I am still in shock that they said yes. Especially after how disastrously my interview went.

After the initial shock lessens a bit, I start thinking about the implications of all of it. It's going to be so much work. What if they want to start right away? They probably do. And I still have so many other jobs waiting in line. What have I been thinking, working all day on a project that isn't for a client? It hasn't been the nearest fire to put out at all.

"Oh my goodness," I say in a new type of daze brought on by realizing all this entails. "I'm going to have to hire an assistant."

Peyton's eyebrows shoot up as she whisks something cooking in a pot. "It's that big of a job? That's exciting!"

It is. I know I can't work out of the dining room of the inn forever, and this isn't exactly going to be what I need to open my own shop, but it is a very big stride toward my goal. I need to start planning.

I pick up my phone to type in some notes about all the things that are coming at my brain, rapid-fire, but stop when I see all of the notifications. How long has it been since I last looked at my phone?

I scroll down the long list. Some are just from social media. Quite a few are texts. Several are from stores telling me about a sale or that I can get $2 off a lunch entree. Some calendar items. Oh. A reminder to pay my credit card bill. I cannot forget that again. Ooh! And a notification from Chat Match.

"My profile has been approved!" I say and go right into it. Peyton takes the pot off the stove and hurries around the island to join me at the table. "Okay, it says to swipe up to read more about each person. I double-tap if I like them and swipe down if I want to dump them out of my list of potential matches. All right. Let's do this."

I click *Okay* on the message, and the first profile pops up. I have used dating apps before, and I am so used to seeing a picture of the guy as the first thing that this feels weird. A row of five icons is at the top, and each one represents the five personality traits I am hoping for in a match. For any where he also lists that he has those personality traits, they light up green. Then right below that is the guy's bio, and below that is how serious a relationship he is looking for. I can even see a full list of his personality traits at the bottom.

Still, though, it doesn't feel like enough. I usually look at the full package before making any decisions and then focus on his face to see if he looks kind and easygoing. Not having that makes me feel like I'm trying to shower and get ready for the day with my eyes closed.

"That guy has three of your things," Peyton says, then reads the man's bio out loud. "'Love dogs? Me, too. We just might be soul mates. Message me to discuss.'"

"That's it? That's the entire bio?" I scroll down, but it really is it. The guy doesn't even choose all twelve of his personality traits. This is impossible. I swipe down.

Brevity isn't a problem for the next guy, though. It looks like a bullet-pointed resume of his skills, accomplishments, and talents. Curious about how long it is, I scroll all the way down. Apparently, the app has a limit on the size of the bio, because it cuts off mid-sentence. I swipe down again.

Then I read the next one out loud. "'Reasons you should date me: One, I can quote at least one line from pretty much any movie ever. Two, I don't have a criminal record. Three, I can make minute rice in fifty-eight seconds.'" I laugh and double-tap on his.

"Really?" Peyton says. "Why?"

I shrug. "He made me laugh."

One of the first things the next guy talks about is his Bentley. I can't swipe down fast enough.

"Okay, why did you swipe down on that one?"

"He was bragging about being rich. Rich guys are jerks."

"All of them? Or just the ones who brag about it?"

"All of them. Maybe I should've put that in my bio. 'If you're rich, save us both some heartache and just swipe down on me immediately.'"

Peyton is quiet for several moments as I go through each profile as they come up. I can feel her eyes on me, though. Finally, Peyton says, "Who hurt you?"

The question is so earnest and blunt that, for some reason, it makes me laugh. "Well, I can tell you that the guy I swiped down on won't!"

Peyton is still looking at me with those sweet, caring eyes, though, so I answer her question for real. "My first real boyfriend, Jack. I knew the Jack he was before his family had money and the Jack he was after, and it was a night-and-day difference. After his family's business took off, he did everything he could to make me feel inferior about my own family's humble situation. Plus," I shrug, "a couple of my mom's boyfriends when I was growing up. I mean, they were all jerks, really, but the two with money were the biggest jerks of all."

Peyton nods like she understands, so I go through a

couple dozen more profiles. Some are awful. Some are good. Some are boring. But at least I get used to the format after a while. In fact, I am starting to get a lot more out of each of the men's bios than I have with any other dating app. Maybe it isn't as hard to go without a picture as I thought.

"Ooh, here's one," I say, seeing a guy who has four of the five icons in green at the top. "'The first thing people notice about me: My nice ears.' Weird, but I like it. 'Four things I can't live without: The cleaner who irons my shirts so I don't have to, the day planner in my phone, my morning routine, and cold cereal with cartoons.' Organized and fun. That's good. 'What I love the most: My family (parents, two sisters, and a brother).'"

"Aww, that's sweet!" Peyton says.

I nod. "'More about me: I'm in international business, love helping kids learn to read, and I can shower in seven minutes flat. If you like movies, cheese, or traveling, we should chat. If you like all three, we should definitely meet in person at some point.'" I immediately double-tap on the guy and cross my fingers that he will double-tap on me so we can start chatting. I really want to ask about those ears. Oh! It is even 4:11. So that is a great sign.

As I scroll through more profiles, Peyton goes back around to the stove and starts cooking something else. "So, how are you going to find an assistant? Do you already have someone in mind?"

"I can't believe I got so distracted I forgot about that!" I close out of the app and go into my notes app—the thing I opened my phone for in the first place. I don't have any idea who to hire. All I know is that it is going to take a lot of focus to pull everything off, and if I don't start making lists, then I'll likely get distracted again and forget half of the vitally important things.

So, even though a Chat Match notification pops up on my screen, I clear it off without even looking to see what it is.

CHAPTER 6

Jackson

I **GET** the notification that my Chat Match profile is live during one of the final planning meetings for my trip to Delhi, and my phone has been burning a hole in my pocket ever since. The meeting lasts over two hours, and I am barely making it back to my office for the first time since lunch.

I glance at the clock on my computer screen as I sit down. 4:13, so I have seventeen minutes until my last meeting of the day. Seventeen minutes to go through some profiles and hopefully find someone to at least chat with, maybe date, and preferably be in a long-term relationship with. Like until-death-do-you-part kind of long.

But, really, I'll settle for someone to chat with while I'm halfway around the world. As I read the screen explaining how to go through the profiles, I amend my lower goal to settling for someone I double-tap on to double-tap on me as well.

I double-tap on a few that make me smile and a few that sound like I would get along with them. I roll my eyes at a few that are over-the-top or so generic that they could've been anyone. And I scratch my head at a few really short bios that I guess might be a quote from a TV show or a song or something that I don't get.

Then I come across one that catches my attention. *Hater of to-do lists.* Why do I find that so attractive? I love them, so being attracted to a self-proclaimed hater of them surprises me. She has to be creative if she is a costume designer. I chuckle at her comment about burning everything she cooks.

It sounds like she is short, which for some reason reminds me of my high school girlfriend, Minnie. I really liked her, and the nostalgic feelings spill over to this woman's profile. Plus, this woman loves tacos. That is definitely a good sign. And the number one, apparently.

I find myself cradling the phone as I scour her profile. The personality traits icons at the top are mostly lit up green. That is also a good sign. The relationship meter isn't over as far as mine is, but she is at least open to casual dating.

I scroll down like I will be able to find more information about her if I just try scrolling past the end, but, of course, there is nothing else.

"Knock, knock. Are you ready for the team meeting? They're all waiting for us to share what we discussed yesterday."

The sound of Ramesh's voice startles me out of a focus on this other world that apparently has been so deep I've forgotten where I am. As my attention jerks up to Ramesh, I fumble my phone. It tumbles and I grab for it, managing to catch it before it clatters to the floor.

But just as I do, my thumb runs across my screen, swiping down on the profile of the woman that I've found so intriguing, and it disappears.

I want to shout, "Nooooooo!" to the sky. But instead, I look at Ramesh and force a smile. "Sorry, yeah. Um, confer-ence room, right?" I glance at the clock. Am I really already late?

"Yeah. But hey, I understand that you've probably got a lot on your mind before you leave tomorrow. If you'd rather cancel…"

"No," I say, placing my phone to the side like it isn't the source of every thought on my mind at the moment. "The meeting's fine. We've got last-minute stuff we need to discuss. Can you give me five minutes and I'll be in?"

Ramesh nods and leaves, and I grab my phone again, trying to see if there is some way to get the woman's profile to come back. But I can't find anything.

And it's not like I can Google to see if there is a way—it is a brand-new app that isn't even available outside the test group in the Portland area.

But Roman has let me know that he wants me to tell him if I find any issues with the app. And this is definitely an issue. An issue that is going to sound really stupid when I tell him, but an issue nonetheless.

I call Roman and nearly hang up while it's ringing. He and I don't know each other super well—we have never socialized outside of business functions. And Roman has given me a way to submit issues I find to the developers, so I shouldn't be taking this issue directly to the CEO of the company. But before I fully decide to hang up, Roman answers. I say, "Please tell me there's a way to get back to a profile that I accidentally swiped down on."

Roman chuckles. "Got in the habit of swiping down and then noticed something promising in one just as you swiped down?"

"Nope. Noticed *lots* of promising things in one, but my co-worker startled me and I dropped the phone. The act of catching it swiped down."

Roman chuckles again. "There's some bad luck for you. The free version doesn't allow you to go back to previous profiles—only the premium one does."

"Please tell me the premium one is available."

"It's still a little too glitchy for beta testers."

My heart sinks—until I hear the next words that come out of Roman's mouth.

"But if you're willing to test a product not ready for the public, I can give you access. You just have to let my developers know about any issues you find."

"No problem. Anything you need."

"I'll send you an access code right now. You'll find a place in the app settings to enter it." He pauses for a moment and then says, "That must be an amazing woman you found."

"I think she might be."

I put in the access code as I am hurrying down the hall toward my meeting. The moment it's in, I feel a release of tension. I will be able to find her again.

The moment I walk into my apartment after work, I pull

my phone out and go into the Chat Match app. I hesitate a moment, though. What if I find her profile again but she never double-taps on me, so I never get to know more about her?

I'll just have to keep my fingers crossed.

The app now has left and right arrows at the bottom—I can scroll through profiles without double-tapping or swiping down. I press the back button. As much as her bio has been burned into my brain, I can't believe that I didn't pay as much attention to her name. It's something different. It starts with a T and has a lot of i's in it.

I find it within seconds. *Timini.* I like it. I double-tap quickly before anything else can go wrong. Immediately, a message pops up that reads, *You matched! Send a message?*

A grin spreads all the way across my face. She *did* double-tap on me. I tap the *Send message* button and immediately wish I had spent the drive home thinking about what to say to her instead of mentally going through my list of things to pack, trying to think of anything I've forgotten and planning exactly what time I will get each of my trip preparations done.

I decide to go for the obvious.

> Jackson: So you're a taco savant. I had
> Taco Sabroso for lunch. Any guess on how
> my afternoon went, based solely on that?

I don't want to stare at my phone, hoping she will respond soon, so I turn my sound on, volume up, set it on the counter, and walk away. I am leaving the country bright and early in the morning and I need to pack, after all.

I make it as far as my bedroom door when I hear the ding from a notification and run back to my phone.

Timini: It depends. What kind did you get?

Jackson: One carnitas and one al pastor.

Timini: Then you walked away with a smile on your face and a bounce in your step. That little feeling of longing in the pit of your stomach that slowed you down about three o'clock was because you didn't also get a fish taco. The combination of all three at Taco Sabroso basically gives you superpowers.

Jackson: So I take it you've had the combination before?

Timini: Just once. I was able to leap over tall buildings in a single jump. But I'm not going to lie—trying to stick the landing while wearing heels wasn't pretty.

Jackson: I see now that eating all three takes advance planning.

Timini: I was there with my sister and two of her kids once when she ate all three. It really freaked them out when she turned invisible, so you definitely want to warn whoever you go with.

I find myself grinning through the conversation and just wanting it to continue.

Jackson: I see that you're a cookie connoisseur. Have you found any of those that also grant superpowers?

Timini: There's a restaurant on Belmont that has cookies with smoked almond, salted caramel, and chocolate chips. They make you good at math. I get one every time I have to pay my bills.

Jackson: That's handy. How long does the math skill last?

Timini: About as long as it takes to feel the sugar crash, so you've got to be ready to use it.

I message back and forth with Timini for hours, throwing my entire planned schedule out the window. The funny thing is, I'm not even sad about that. Even though normally, it would drive me nuts not to be keeping up with my schedule down to the minute. *Especially* on the night before such an important and long trip.

I love that she is so playful. That isn't a trait I have seen in a woman I've met in my own circles since college, probably. It is awakening a playful part of myself that has lain dormant for far too long.

At eleven p.m., I finally decide we need to say goodnight —I have to be at the airport at five a.m., and I got almost no packing done while we chatted.

It has been worth it, though. Even though Timini and I haven't talked about anything of substance yet. We've just had fun chatting. I have learned a few things about her, though. That she is five foot one inch (if she is currently "thinking really tall thoughts"), which is a full ten inches shorter than me. Unless, she points out, she is wearing heels. Then it is more like a six-inch difference.

I also learned that her favorite food is anything someone else cooked, which I could have guessed from her bio. When I pressed for something more specific, she mentioned Mexican food. Then Thai. Then Chinese. Then pizza. Then cheesecake. Then Italian. Eventually, she said she just really liked food, to which I replied that—surprise!—I really did too. So she said it was such a coincidence that we must be soul mates, and I laughed so hard that every neighbor of mine on this floor probably heard me.

By the end of our chat, I am dying to ask for her number, or her last name, or to follow her on social media, but I force the thought away. If I ask it of her, she will want the same from me, and that will ruin everything.

No. Now is the time to just enjoy communicating with someone I am really connecting to. I need a chance to really get to know her before introducing things like who my family is into the mix.

Timini

I PUT a bag of popcorn in the microwave, push the popcorn button, and then look up at the cupboard above the microwave where we keep the big popcorn bowl. Sure, near the microwave makes sense for a popcorn bowl, but does it have to be up so high? I am currently barefoot and literally can't even reach the knob to open the door, let alone reach anything inside.

I turn to where my roommates are all chatting and snacking on the cheese and vegetable trays before we move into the family room to watch a movie. "Ian, can you help me?"

He comes around the island, opens the door, and gets out the bowl with no problem at all before handing it to me. "How can you handle being so short? Does it drive you nuts?"

"Hey," I say. "There are benefits to being short."

Addison just smiles, like she knows what's coming, but

Ian looks like he doesn't believe that I am actually going to be able to come up with a list. So I start laying it out for him, ticking each one off on my fingers. "I always have all the legroom I need. I can wear high heels all I want. I get to be in the front of group pictures. I never hit my head on things. I can move through a crowd like no one's business. Short people have less of a risk of cancer."

"You're making that one up," Roman says.

I shake my head. "I'm not—look it up. We also live longer and get fewer blood clots. Oh, and I totally killed it at hide-and-seek when I was a kid."

"So you've always been short?" Ian asks. "You didn't hit five feet—"

"Five feet one inch," I correct.

"My apologies. You didn't hit five foot one in third grade and just decided to stop growing right then and there?"

I shake my head and grab a carrot stick. "I've been the shortest kid in every single school class I've been in. I hadn't even hit the five-foot mark when I started high school. In fact, I didn't even go by 'Timini' back then."

At everyone's confused faces, I explain. "Even though the last part of my name is said 'muh-nee,' it's spelled 'mini,' and, because I am short and kids are kids, that's what everyone started calling me. But by fourth grade, it was clear 'mini' wasn't going away anytime soon, so instead of fighting it, I embraced it and just became 'Minnie,' and spelled it M-I-N-N-I-E. It was my dad who chose my unusual name, and I'd been mad at the fact that I'd never even met him, so I had no problem changing it. I even got my mom and sister to call me that."

Well, I didn't exactly get my mom to call me "Minnie" as much as she called me "Mini Me." It annoyed me, but at least it was close to Minnie. Eventually, my mom dropped the "Me" part of it and just called me Minnie when I was an adult and finally caught up to her (also short) height. She never switched back to calling me Timini, though, once I did. Maybe because she was still mad at my dad, too.

"And then, I made my mom go to the school and have them add the 'goes by' name to their rolls so that at the beginning of each new year, I wouldn't have to have the teacher call roll and say 'Timini' just for me to correct them and say, 'Actually, I go by Minnie.' It was the only name I went by until I got to college and decided it was time to take 'Timini' back." I stick the carrot in my mouth and take a bite.

"How did we not know this?" Bex asks. "Seriously, girl, you went by a different name for, what? Nine years?"

I shrug and take another bite. "I also had braces for four excruciatingly long years, and I've never told you that, either."

"True," Peyton says, "but your beautiful teeth told that story for you."

"It was a long time ago. I've been Timini again for ten years."

The smell of something burning hits my nose. How have I missed the microwave beeping? I run to it, throw the door wide, and open the top of the bag as I'm pulling it out so the heat can escape and quit trying to burn the beautiful popcorn inside. I dump it in the bowl to let it cool even more quickly.

"Well, at least it was only a little part that burnt instead of the whole bag," I say as I pick the blackened pieces out of the bowl.

"So," Roman says, "not to talk shop at a friend get-together or anything, but how is Chat Match going? Any issues or suggestions?"

I can actually feel my cheeks warm as I pick the last few blackened kernels out of the bowl. I never blush. "It's going well," I say to the bowl, just to give my cheeks a chance to return to normal.

"Have you met any good guys?" I can hear the grin in Peyton's voice.

Okay, I am probably in the clear with the cheeks now, so I turn around and put the bowl of popcorn next to the other snack foods. "I've been chatting with a handful of guys, actually."

"Oh yeah?" Addison asks. "And what did you think?"

"One guy was pretty chatty. I felt like he was super honest and authentic, which was nice. He even shared his feelings. He was an open book."

"All good stuff," Ian says. "Is it looking like it will go anywhere?"

I shake my head. "He is an open book, but the book just isn't very thick. It's more like a pamphlet."

Bex laughs loudly.

"There is one guy I matched with, so I sent him a message but he never responded."

"Well," Peyton says, "obviously he was so excited to hear from you that he fainted."

This time, I'm the one who laughs. "Yeah, I'm sure that's it. There was another guy yesterday who asked me to go on a date with him within five minutes of saying, 'Hi,' and I responded with, 'I'm excited to meet you in a busy, well-lit area.' Because we hadn't gotten to know each other well enough to *not* make that part clear. Things fizzled out with him pretty quickly."

"Any good ones you've been talking with?" Bex asks, and I swear she is doing it because she saw the blush and is trying to bring it back. She might just succeed.

"One." And there's the blush again that apparently that has only ever been absent in my life when we're not talking about Jackson. "His name is Jackson, and he's so much fun to talk to. We chatted for more than four hours last night."

"Four hours!" Peyton says.

I just smile. It was long enough that going all day without talking to him has actually been hard. I'm fairly certain that I can't miss someone I've only known for four hours, but I do a little bit. Oh, and look at that—it's seven-oh-one. It's about the tenth number one I have seen today, and I'd been thinking of Jackson when seeing each of them. That has to mean something.

Peyton cocks her ear toward the doorway, hearing a sound that I swear only her ears are tuned to hear. "Oh! Max is here!" She runs toward the front of the inn to greet him.

"And?" Bex says. "How much have you talked to him today?"

"Not at all." I try to not show how sad that makes me. "He hopped on a plane to Delhi early this morning, and it's a twenty-four-hour flight."

"Ouch," Max says as he and Peyton join us, hand-in-hand, looking like adorable little lovebirds. "Long flight."

It is long for me, too.

"Okay," Addison says, picking up the cheese tray, "let's get this party started!"

We all head out of the kitchen and into the lobby, walking under part of the paper chain that goes over the doorway and has one link representing each day until Peyton and Max get married—fifty-one left!—toward the family room.

Then, I hear the notification sound that only comes from Chat Match. I race back into the room, looking around at all the tables I've been moving between as I worked today. Where did I leave my phone? I knew Jackson couldn't message me, so I haven't been keeping track of it. Logic tells me that it isn't him now, either—he still has many hours to go before his plane lands—but I can't bring myself to ignore that notification.

I lift up so much fabric, and soon Bex and Peyton are helping me. Roman must've recognized the sound the notification made, because he just stands, leaning against the door frame, grinning. Probably because his company made the thing that is causing me to lose my mind.

I tell myself that it is probably just one of the other guys messaging. Which is totally fine. I am having fun chatting with them, too. Not as much fun as with Jackson, of course.

"Got it!" Bex shouts, holding it up in triumph.

I run to the phone and look at the screen. "Aww! It's from Jackson!" With as much as I've thought about him today, I shouldn't be surprised at how thrilled it makes me to see his name. It especially thrills me because I thought I wouldn't for many hours. I swipe to open it. Maybe he is on a layover, waiting.

Jackson: I've got a riddle for you. What do you call a guy who has spent the day working 35,000 feet in the air, doing it all without in-flight WiFi, then breaks down and buys it at the end of the day just to send a message to a girl he met twenty-four hours ago and has never laid eyes on?

Timini: I'd call him a smart man with very good timing.

Jackson: Ooh. Tell me more about this "good timing" I have.

I make my way to the family room and hurry to claim the comfiest chair. It only fits one person, so it's not like anyone else is going to claim it, but still. It feels like a victory when I act like I have to race for it. I tuck my feet up under me on the chair, and then I respond to Jackson.

Timini: We are having TV night with my 3 best friends and their 2 husbands and 1 fiancé.

Jackson: Ahh. So I'm the virtual date so that you won't be a 7th wheel.

Jackson: Wait. You don't have a date there, do you? Am I crashing the date, making me...what? The 9th wheel? Does that metaphor even make sense after about the number five?

Timini: I don't have a date already. Want to be mine for the next little bit? Or is it too soon to move from chatting to dating? And semis have 18 wheels, so I'm pretty sure you can use the metaphor up to 19.

Jackson: I'd love to be your date for the evening.

Jackson: And if this feels too fast, we can just promise not to kiss at the end of the date. Heck, let's say no arm around the shoulder, no holding hands, nothing. Hands and lips to ourselves. Deal?

Timini: You drive a hard bargain, but I promise not to kiss you or try to hold your hand.

Jackson: I might be a little underdressed— I'm wearing worn jeans and a T-shirt. What are we doing for said date?

Timini: You're not underdressed. In fact, if you're on a twenty-four-hour flight, you're clearly overdressed. This is the kind of situation where you wear sweats. And it's "Unsolicited Advice Night" over here. It's where we watch the show "Flip My House, Not My Life," and shout out what we think they should do and not do. Have you seen it?

Jackson: That's the show where they completely renovate a house while the owners are still living in it, right? I haven't seen it, but I've heard about it.

Timini: That's the one. Oh, and we place "bragging rights" bets on whether or not the couple will still be married by the recap.

Jackson: Ouch. The remodels are that rough?

Timini: Yes. This is the show where you learn how to do home improvements, and also learn to NEVER do them if you value your relationship with the people in your home.

Jackson: That should be their slogan, right there. Which episode are we watching?

I look up to find all six of my roommates—well, five plus one who will be a roommate soon enough—watching me. Like I'm the entertainment for the night.

"What? Did I miss something?"

Ian says, "Nah," at the same time Roman says, "We were just asking if you were ready to start," and Peyton says, "We were just enjoying watching you fall for a guy on the dating app."

"I'm not falling for him!" But if I think about it for two seconds, I know it's a lie. My stomach gets all fluttery with every message from him that comes in. "Okay, maybe I am a little. But he's out of the country for three weeks. And it's not like you can really tell if you're falling for someone before you see them in real life. He's just fun to chat with, and he's going to be my date for the evening. And it's not like he's the only guy I'm chatting with. What episode are we on?"

Okay, normally when I go on an occasional date, I only get excited about their looks and never the conversations I have with them. So maybe this is something different than my usual. It explains why my roommates are all giving me looks of barely concealed glee that I am thoroughly ignoring right now.

"Season two, episode four," Addison says, and I let Jackson know.

> **Jackson:** I'm pulling it up right now.

> **Timini:** Right now. While you're on a plane.

> **Jackson:** Yep. Flying over the Atlantic. Tell me when to press play.

We start the show, and everyone immediately begins giving their unsolicited advice. The couple has only been married for six months, so from the start, we all think it's a bad idea and are vocal about it. The wife is open to half the house being remodeled—the kitchen and bathrooms. The husband wants it all done. Every square inch.

Both spouses make their share of bad choices that even the contractor gives them unsolicited advice on. (I can understand the wife wanting double sinks in the master bathroom. But double toilets? In the same room? And I can't understand even a little why the husband wants built-in shelf-like padded seats going all the way around all four walls in their family room instead of having furniture that they can move.)

It is a great episode. All of my roommates give the funniest advice to the couple. I type a lot of it in messages to Jackson, along with my own advice, and he types back plenty of his own funny advice.

I've brought dates to group things before. Never, though, has my date joined in with the group so seamlessly. It's nice. I'm so used to feeling like the odd man out on group dates, but I don't feel like that at all tonight.

> Jackson: Thank you for the enjoyable date. I can't say I've ever gone on one while on a plane, with someone I've never met in person, especially not a group date with six of her roommates.

> Timini: I'm guessing you thought all your first dates with women from this app were going to be predictable.

> Jackson: That's some pro-level mind-reading right there. Wait. You didn't get the super-power-granting trio of tacos without me, did you?

> Timini: It was the cheese tray that granted me mind-reading capabilities, actually.

> Jackson: What am I thinking right now?

Timini: That they turned down the lights in the cabin, so they clearly want you all to go to sleep. And you're feeling a little guilty that you have a bright screen that's probably annoying your seatmate. So you should go, but you'd really rather stay up for hours, chatting with me.

Timini: But also, part of you just wants to fall unconscious right now, since we stayed up so late last night, chatting, and you had to get up so early. And you're landing in a country that's already half a day ahead of you, so sleeping sounds like the responsible thing to do.

Jackson: It's astounding how correct you are.

Timini: #Pro

Jackson: You're going to have to introduce me to this cheese when I get back.

Timini: I wouldn't miss the chance. Have a safe flight! Get good sleep.

Jackson: Will do. Goodnight, Timini.

I close out of the app and sink back into my comfy chair, happiness filling me. Never did I imagine that a virtual date with someone who is practically a stranger would leave me feeling so amazing.

CHAPTER 8

Jackson

AFTER AN EXTREMELY LONG DAY—MY first full day in Delhi—I finally get back to my room. I got a few messages earlier in the day from people I matched with, but I didn't even have a small moment to respond until now.

Responding, though, doesn't give me a fraction of the high I get from talking with Timini. I glance at the clock on my phone. It's nearly nine p.m. for me, but that puts Oregon at almost seven-thirty a.m., and I suddenly realize that I have no idea what time Timini normally wakes up.

I send her a good morning message through the app, hoping that the notification won't wake her up if she isn't ready to be awake yet. But also really hoping she is already up because, after such a long day, I really just want to see words with her name next to them.

Timini: Good morning!

> Timini: Oh. It's probably not morning for you, is it? It isn't the middle of the night, is it?

> Jackson: Nope. I'm thirteen and a half hours ahead.

> Timini: "And a half." Interesting. I'm guessing what you've gotten done today has to be way more impressive than what I've gotten done. Especially since all I've done is wander into the bathroom to see how messy my hair is.

I suddenly want to know exactly what Timini looks like with messy hair. Or with any kind of hair.

> Timini: How was your first full day there?

> Jackson: I went to half a dozen meetings at three different locations. I got to ride their train (the metro), a rickshaw (which is a vehicle that comfortably seats a person and a half and only has one wheel in the front), and a taxi. And today I learned that you're supposed to negotiate a fare with the driver BEFORE driving an inch. I know that now.

> Timini: Uh oh.

> Jackson: It's all good. And this place is amazing. It just bombards you with all the sights, sounds, smells, people, culture, art, and food. Oh, and the heat.

Timini: That sounds INCREDIBLE.

Jackson: Were you referring to the heat or the rest of it?

Timini: All of it.

Jackson: You're a fan of hot weather, huh?

Timini: The hotter the better.

Jackson: This place resembles an oven. You would love it.

Timini: Clearly, I'll have to go there sometime. Now tell me about the food you've eaten.

Jackson: I tried Thali, which is a flatbread that you use to scoop up chickpeas in a sauce. And also Chat, which the guy told me will pretty much give me superpowers that rival the taco combo at Taco Sabroso. And I managed to get out of eating the goat brain, so I'm calling it a win.

Timini: Now I'm hungry. I think I'll wander downstairs and find some food.

I picture her making her way down to the kitchen and opening the fridge door, and I really want to see her. To know what she looks like.

But I also really want to spend time finding out more about her.

> Timini: Do you travel out of the country often?

> Jackson: Only 2-3 times a year. And then a handful of times in the country a year.

> Timini: What's the most memorable place you've been?

> Jackson: Guatemala. It wasn't for business, though. It was the summer after high school, and I was building houses for struggling villages. It was literally a life-changing experience.

Timini sends the emoji with heart eyes, and I suddenly want to know everything I can about her.

> Jackson: I feel like we've gotten to know each other's personality pretty well but I don't feel like I really know who you are. What do you say to us asking each other questions? You know, to dive in deeper.

> Timini: Oh. Like whether or not I put my toothbrush under the water before I put toothpaste on it? Because I'm going to tell you right now that putting toothpaste on a dry toothbrush is just plain weird. We're talking deal-breaker territory.

I laugh out loud. Then I leap onto my bed, landing stretched out on my side and propped up on one elbow.

Jackson: See? I already feel like I know you more deeply.

I look up at the ceiling, trying to think of what I want to ask. With more than half a day time difference between the two of us for the next eighteen days, I realize I want to know when she might be awake.

Jackson: Are you a morning person or a night owl?

Timini: A night owl, FOR SURE. I start working at an okay time in the mornings. Usually. I mean, depending on your opinion, I guess. I went to bed at a decent time last night. But night is when all my best ideas come. Sometimes, I get working on a project and suddenly realize it's 3 a.m. You?

Jackson: I can't say I have that same issue. Like, ever. I'm an early bird. Up at exactly six. I have a morning routine. It feels like a game that I've already figured out my high score on, so I try to reach that same high score daily.

Timini: That sounds like a SUPER fun game.

Then she sends a text with the emoji of the yellow circle-faced guy raising one eyebrow, probably so I won't take her comment seriously.

> Timini: You sound like you're very consistent with your bedtimes. How is the time difference treating you?

> Jackson: Ask me tomorrow. That's when the crash usually hits. Right now I'm doing just fine.

Although I shouldn't be just lounging around like I am. I met with several investors, potential manufacturers, and a potential retailer today. I should be typing up my notes and sending them back to the office because they probably want to discuss them today. And I should be preparing for my meetings tomorrow.

It isn't like me to just blow it all off so that I can message a woman on a dating app. But nothing about Timini is making me want to do what I normally do.

> Jackson: What is the one thing you most regret?

> Timini: Oh, wow. You're really going straight for the vulnerability topics, aren't you?

> Jackson: Go big or go home, right?

> Timini: It couldn't be just something I regret? It has to be what I MOST regret? Because I regret not having donuts waiting in the kitchen for me for breakfast.

> Jackson: Well, I guess it depends on how deep of an answer you want from me.

Timini: You do know how to sweeten the deal. Okay, fine. What I most regret. But I'm swearing you to secrecy because this isn't something I share with people.

I send her the emoji of the little yellow face with the zipped lips.

Timini: My biggest regret is not finishing college. I went for two years and fully planned to go for four. But then I got the opportunity to intern for a year with a giant in the field of costume design, and I couldn't pass it up. She let me work with her full-time, and I at least doubled everything I had learned about costume-making from my entire life up until that point. She helped me get going on my own, helped me make connections, and recommended me to several people in the industry.

Timini: Doing this on my own—with running my own shop on the horizon—is only possible because of that internship. But when it finished, I had to make a choice. Instead of going back to college, I chose to run with the momentum I gained in that internship and started out on my own.

Jackson: And you regret that?

Timini: Yeah. It feels unfinished. But if it was only that, it would be okay, because I feel like I made the decision with my eyes open. It's whenever "What college did you graduate from?" comes up in conversation that I most regret it. Not being able to say that I graduated makes me feel inconsequential. Not capable of finishing things. Like I wasn't smart enough to do it. I avoid the conversation at all costs because it always makes me feel like a loser.

Jackson: From everything I know of you, I can certify that you're not a loser. You just finished your education in a different way. If you'd like, I can make you a very official-looking graduation certificate. You can have it framed and hang it on the wall of your future design shop.

Timini: I'll take it! Okay, your turn, Mister.

Jackson: Mine happened in middle school, the class right after lunch. Our teacher was late getting back so we were all just waiting in the hallway outside the classroom for the door to be unlocked. There was a kid in my class who was brilliant but socially awkward. A few of the other kids stood right in front of him, making fun of everything about his appearance from his hair to his freckles to his too-short pants and "not cool" shoes.

Jackson: My biggest regret is not stepping in to defend him. I could've asked them to stop. Physically stepped between the kid and his attackers. Put my arm around the kid and led him away. Turned their attention on me. Anything. But I didn't—I just stood there. I felt bad about it for weeks. I still do, actually. I think about that often. I made a promise to myself from that point on to always step in and defend someone whenever they needed me to.

Timini sends me the emoji that has hearts for eyes, but it doesn't feel earned when I just shared something I don't like that I did. Or, in this case, didn't do. A few moments later, she sends a message that catches me off guard.

Timini: So...do you think we should exchange pictures so we have a face to go with the names and winning personalities?

Timini: Or should we not and keep the magic going?

It makes me smile that she wants to know more about me just like I want to know more about her. Part of me wants to type a quick YES! A big enough part that I have to try hard to stop myself and truly think about it first. I want to see Timini.

The entire reason I agreed to use this app, though—especially at a time when I literally can't see any matches in person—is because I want to know if there is someone out there with relationship potential. Someone who won't just like me because of what they can Google about me or my family. I want a relationship that goes beyond the superficial things.

> Jackson: As much as I want to see you, I kind of like the magic.

> Timini: OH GOOD. As soon as I asked, I wished I hadn't. I like it, too.

> Timini: Do you make your bed in the morning?

I laugh. When I picture us getting to know each other further, I haven't been sure what questions to ask that won't lead to asking about each other's families. I haven't imagined us talking about bedmaking or teeth brushing or sleeping patterns. But this is perfect.

> Jackson: Always. Before I leave my room. There's an admiral who says that if you do that first thing, the momentum created by getting that task done will help you accomplish more in a day.

> Timini: Yeah, I never really got that. There are lots of things you can do in the morning to feel accomplished. I would never choose the one that made the least sense.

> Jackson: How does making your bed not make sense? If you do it, then your sheets and blankets are all straight and ready for you when you go to bed.

Timini: Nah. Made beds look off-limits and intimidating. Unmade beds look comfy. I don't want to get to my room at the end of a tiring day and feel like I can't even get under the covers.

The thought of crawling into an unmade bed isn't a pleasant one. Yet I love how unapologetically herself Timini is, and it helps me at least understand her perspective.

For the next week, every evening when I get home from a packed, exhausting day, I message Timini as she's waking up. And in her evenings, she messages me as I'm waking up. Sometimes we tell each other about our days. Sometimes we banter about inconsequential things. Sometimes we ask each other questions. Funny, serious, shallow, deep, insightful, blunt—I love them all.

I especially love hearing about her job and the new project she's taking on. It's bigger than anything she's done before, and she even hired an assistant to help her. It's exciting to see her business in the beginning stages of it really taking off. I remember hearing my parents talk about their business taking off when I was in elementary school, and it's fun to watch it happen now with Timini.

I end the chats on the app with other women I matched with and push the pause button on my profile. Timini and I haven't even come close to talking about being exclusive, but the only thing I use the app for now is talking to her. It feels like it has always been only about her.

One night as I'm waiting for food in a restaurant, I imagine going on a date with Timini when I return to

Oregon and send her a question, hoping to get some ideas on where to take her.

> Jackson: What was your favorite date you've ever gone on and why?

The second I tap *Send,* I wish I could call it back. It's a stupid question to ask—I really don't want to hear about a date she had with another guy. So I just wait for her answer, turning my phone over and over in my hand, wishing my food would arrive more quickly so I could do something other than wait.

The second I feel the buzz of the notification, I go in to see what she has written.

> Timini: Oh, gosh. I'm going to have to go all the way back to high school for that one. I was going with a guy and a group of friends to a school dance—a casual one at the end of my sophomore year. We went on a "day date" before the dance. Did your school do day dates on the day of dances, too?

> Jackson: We totally did. Dances were an all-day thing.

> Timini: So, like probably half the nation's high school students that year, we decided to do a photo scavenger hunt.

> Jackson: Ahh, yes. The photo scavenger hunt. We did that, too. We thought we were so original back then.

Timini: The reason the date made it to the top of my list wasn't even because of the scavenger hunt, exactly. It was more of the way we connected, I guess. My date just made me feel loved and cared for.

After chatting with Timini for so many hours over the past nine days, hearing that just makes me want to be the person who makes her feel loved and cared for.

Timini: Your turn. What was your favorite date and why?

Her answer about a high school dance takes me back to high school, too, and suddenly I can't think of any date other than those. I dated my girlfriend, Minnie, all of my junior year. We were apparently as original as Timini's group and also decided to go on a photo scavenger hunt. Then we went to dinner, the dance, and then we all went back to my house for a movie on an outdoor screen that my buddies and I set up before the date.

My favorite part, though, was after the movie. All the other couples left, but Minnie and I stayed in the backyard, lying on a blanket in the grass, holding hands in the dark, staring up at the millions of stars overhead.

We talked for the longest time. Minnie told me about her mom's current boyfriend and how terribly he treated her mom yet somehow always made her mom believe that she was the one treating him terribly.

And I told her about how my parents' business was starting to grow so much in such a small amount of time, and how it felt like everything was on the brink of changing.

How scared it made me. I talked about how worried I was that my parents might want our family to move soon, and Minnie said she was worried that her mom would never move on. We shared our hopes and dreams and plans for college, and I had never felt closer to another person before.

> Jackson: My favorite date was in high school, too (junior year for me, though), and it isn't really about what we did for the date, either. We went stargazing (also a super popular date activity in my high school), and what made the date memorable was the conversation, not the stars.

> Jackson: Although the stars did add some great ambiance.

> Timini: So true. Do you have any stars there yet?

I duck in my seat to see under the awning that covers the outdoor seating area. I got through an exhausting day of travel and meetings later than normal, so I'm eating in the dark tonight.

> Jackson: There's a lot of activity going on in this market—too many lights. I'm not sure I've seen any while I've been here. I'll have to check when I get back to my hotel.

> Timini: How much longer are you gone?

I smile at her question. Maybe she wants to see me as badly as I want to see her.

Jackson: 11 more days.

When I left home for this trip, three weeks didn't seem too long to be gone at all. And, really, for all I have to accomplish, it isn't long at all. But the more I chat with Timini, the more I want to meet her in person and the longer it feels like it will be until my trip comes to an end.

CHAPTER 9
Timini

I'M STILL FEELING the euphoria from an incredible date as my high school boyfriend, Jack, walks me up the steps to my front porch. I am still me, but I am also the sixteen-year-old me. A very distinct mix of the Timini I am now and the Minnie I was back then. Jack is still Jack, too, but he somehow feels older.

When we get to my door, we face each other, less than a foot apart. Close enough that I can smell the wintergreen scent of his gum. We talk, but the words are wispy and intangible, drifting away in the wind on ephemeral clouds. Then Jack reaches out, cupping my head with one hand and with the other, brushing the hair away from my face with his fingertips as they skim ever so slightly across my cheek.

The date has been so magical that every nerve tingles in anticipation of his lips against mine. I lean closer to him, letting my eyes drift closed. The moment his lips touch mine, sparkling lights fill my mind. As he so gently, carefully, moves his lips against mine, like I am precious, fragile, of great worth, my knees literally weaken and nearly buckle. He just holds me closer, using his strength to add to mine.

Then he pulls back from the kiss and looks me straight in the eyes, and I sit up in bed with a jolt, gasping. It takes a few minutes of panting before I get my bearings and realize where I am and that I have been dreaming. The dream has been so intense and has felt so real! I fall back onto my pillow, still trying to reclaim my breath and calm my heart rate.

Why in the world am I dreaming about a boyfriend I had a dozen years ago?

It's probably because of that question Jackson asked last night about my favorite date. And I probably only went all the way back to high school for my answer simply because Jackson's name is similar to my high school boyfriend Jack's.

That's all it is. I hadn't thought of that night for so many years that the dream had to have been triggered because of our conversation.

It was a pretty great date. And an even more incredible kiss at the end. We had been dating for most of the school year at that point.

For the photo scavenger hunt, we'd split into teams of two. One of the things we had to get a picture of was a Dumpster. We both thought of the same one—one in an alley between a restaurant and a hair salon. At least one of us had to be in the picture with the object we were searching for, and it was my turn. I crouched down, like I was hiding, just beyond the corner, waiting for someone to come so I could jump out and scare them or something. Jack took the picture, and as I turned to stand, I realized that I had been crouching next to a nest of very large spiders.

I was so freaked out. I screamed, batting at my clothes and hair, worried that they were all over me. Jack was to me in a second, pulling me away from the danger, checking to make sure no spiders were on me, batting away the one that was with his bare hands, and then pulling me to safety and into his chest. His shoulders were strong, and he wrapped his arms around me, holding me tight, whispering promises that I was okay and that no spiders were on me. He didn't rush the moment even though it meant losing the competition.

I felt so loved and cared for. The experience was so different from any of the guys who moved in with my mom, and I knew at that moment what I wanted—a guy who would care for me just like Jack did.

After dinner and the dance, our whole group went to Jack's house for an outdoor movie. We planned to watch a scary one about a cabin in the woods, but the scare from earlier was too fresh, and I worried there might be spiders in the movie. I didn't even have to say a thing; Jack just announced to the group that we were going to watch a different movie. A happier one.

After the movie, when everyone else had gone home, we held hands as we looked up at the stars and talked. I remember thinking how perfect the date was and how much I yearned for a life exactly like that night.

I shake my head as I force myself to a sitting position on my bed. Jack told me that night so long ago that he was worried about everything in his family changing. But it only took a couple of months before *he* changed the most, and that ruined everything. Suddenly I—and my not-so-affluent upbringing—was no longer good enough. My image no longer fit with his new image. I no longer belonged in the world he was suddenly entitled to because of his family's wealth.

The worst part was, the day after I broke up with him, I saw him at Jumping Trolley, a place we all liked to hang out. I was with my friends, and he was with his. My group had to pass by his on the way to our seats, and when we passed, he acted like he was in the middle of a conversation with his friends, but his words were clearly directed at me. "So then the doctor asked her, where does it hurt? And she unlocked her phone and showed him her bank account." And then all his friends laugh.

I shake off the bitter memory and the happy dream. Then I pick up my phone to look at the time and congratulate myself for waking up a full thirty minutes before my alarm is set to go off. So there's something good that came from the dream. It's like a gift of thirty minutes just plopped into my lap, and I smile big.

Then I notice a calendar notification.

"No, no, no!" I say out loud as I go into it. "That can't be today!"

But there, on my calendar, is the appointment I listed for a final fitting for a series of costumes I've been working on. How have I not realized that we are already this far into the month? I need an extra six hours this morning, not an extra thirty minutes.

A week ago, I met with Aftyn Flint, the director I interviewed with at Hamilton Hall. The meeting went well, but I also found out the scope of what I will be doing. Naya, the other director, joined the meeting for a bit, too, and she talked about what she was looking for in the Prince Charming costume. It's an intricate one that will take quite a while just by itself to concept and create.

Over the past week, I've gotten the measurements for all the cast members, got my initial ideas for the costumes approved, posted a job opening for an assistant, interviewed applicants, and hired someone. I am still impressed at all I've gotten done.

What I haven't gotten finished, though, is a set of *Beauty and the Beast* costumes for a middle school play. I've already finished the most difficult pieces with the exception of one dress. It's mostly the costumes for the townspeople that I have left. None are intricate, original, or detailed like the ones for the Williams Theater at Hamilton Hall, but they are still a lot of work.

At least now I have Evie. She is twenty-five. She dropped out of college after her third year of business school, took a few years off, and then figured out that clothing design was her true passion and went back. So I only have her part-time, and she just started yesterday, but already she is a godsend and is keeping me on track.

If only I had thought to tell my new employee about the *Beauty and the Beast* client. Yesterday, when we made a list of all the things that needed to get done for my existing projects and the new ones I just took on, the deadlines for each project, decided how long each one would take, and then plugged it into a calendar, taking both of our work schedules into consideration, I completely forgot about it. I have no idea how. Sure, my processes (until yesterday) have been lacking, but I have never completely forgotten about a project before. Especially a half-finished one.

Well, except that one teeny one last year.

This isn't a huge project, but it also isn't a finish-in-one-day project. We are seriously going to be scrambling to get them ready to try on today, and it's going to throw our entire schedule out of whack.

I send a quick text to Evie, hoping that six thirty-seven isn't too early to text.

> Timini: I forgot about a set of costumes that is due today! If you have any spare time and are willing to work more hours, I will make it up to you somehow. You name it.

> Evie: My 2:00 class just got canceled, so I can work until 4:00 now. I'll be over ASAP!

I breathe a huge sigh of relief as I race into the bathroom. My hair is still in the crazy bun I put it in after showering last night, and it's still a little damp. That is going to have to be good enough—the only thing I have time for today is teeth brushing.

I take the stairs two at a time and race into the kitchen. It doesn't sound like anyone else is even up yet. Hopefully, they are either sleeping deeply or are close to waking up anyway, because I am about to tear through the contents of the six round tables in this dining room and my shelves like a tornado. All of the costumes are started—some just have the pattern made, some are cut out, and some are at least partially sewn. And I need to find them all.

———

Six hours later, Evie and I are both slowing down from the marathon we've been running, even though we aren't close to being finished. Jackson sent me a few messages earlier, just checking in to see how my day was going, and I quickly filled him in on the chaos that is my day. He wished me luck. As much as I would've loved to chat with him, I'm glad he hasn't sent me any other messages because I wouldn't have had a chance to respond.

I just finished sewing a very puffy, multi-layered skirt to a corset—the most difficult part in the costumes we are making today—and hand it off to Evie to pin the fabric that goes from the bust up over the shoulders. Then I move on to doing the finish details on a dress for one of the townspeople.

"This doesn't fit," Evie says. "The top part's too big for the corset."

I look over at Evie's bewildered expression, rather bewildered myself. I go over to the table where she is working with her own sewing machine.

"How? I checked it right before sewing the skirts on!" But I look at the partially sewn top, and it is indeed too big. So I gather up the dress and take it to the same dress form with all the actress's measurements that I tried the corset on before starting on the skirts. I pull the dress onto the form and then try zipping the corset. It only goes halfway up and stops.

I adjust the dress, in case it isn't sitting just right anywhere, but it still won't zip. Then I notice that the base of the corset is looser than it should be.

"Oh, no. Oh, no, oh no." I take the dress off and put it on upside down, with the skirts going up over the lack of a head on the dress form. The corset fits perfectly. "I just sewed that entire skirt on the wrong side of the corset!"

"So what do we do?" Evie glances from the dress to the clock on the wall.

I put a hand on my forehead. It's 2:11, and the cast is coming for the fitting at three. Two ones in the time—that has to mean something good, but nothing here looks good. We are behind more than we can possibly make up at this point. "I have no idea. It'll take an hour to unstitch this and another thirty minutes to sew it back on correctly. We don't have that kind of time."

Not to mention that we are both fading fast. Probably because we haven't eaten anything all day. Evie's stomach is growling as loudly as mine is.

At the sound of a notification on my phone, I go back to my table to look at it, hoping for some kind of miracle. Like the school saying they can't actually come for the fitting until tomorrow.

Instead, it's a message from Jackson.

> Jackson: Has the chaos died down at all?
> How are things going?

> Timini: They are going SO BAD.

Jackson: Have you eaten?

Timini: No.

Jackson: You'll work more quickly if you do.

Timini: I know. But there's no time to make anything. No time to even order anything.

Jackson: Do you have time to answer the door?

I've barely read the message when the doorbell rings. My brows come together, and I walk out of the dining room to the lobby, my phone still in my hand, the dating app still open. I reach out and pull the door open, and standing on my porch, under cover from the rain that is drizzling, is a guy in a Taco Sabroso shirt, holding a bag.

"Are you Timini?"

I nod.

"Someone really, *really* wanted you to have these tacos today. Enjoy."

I take the bag from the man and try to pay him, but he says that the bill—and a sizeable tip—are already covered.

As I take the bag into the kitchen, a sense of wonder fills my entire body. Has Jackson seriously ordered me food from Taco Sabroso and arranged to have it delivered, all the way from Delhi, India?

After setting the bag on the big dining table, I take out the first food container—the one with my name on it—and open it. It contains three tacos: one carnitas, one al pastor, and one fish. I suddenly realize how famished I am, and a tear nearly escapes my eye as I think about how sweet Jackson is to do this.

The second box has *Timini's Assistant* written on top of it, and it contains the same three tacos. He's even thought of my assistant! I hand Evie the one for her and then send a message to Jackson.

Timini: I can't believe you did this for me! How did you even know where to have it delivered?

Jackson: That was a gamble. You told me you lived in an inn that was no longer an inn in Quicksand, so I did some research and some finger-crossing. I figured if there was a day when you needed superpowers, it was today.

Jackson: And here's hoping that they give you super speed or time travel, and not one of the ones that wouldn't be so useful in this situation, like the ability to speak any language or fly or indestructibility or animal transformation.

Jackson: Telekinesis or object manipulation might even be good.

Timini: I know we haven't met in person, but if you were here right now, I would kiss you.

Jackson: And if I were there, I would probably let you.

Timini: Only probably? ;)

> Jackson: I wouldn't want to keep you or your forthcoming superpowers from pulling off a fourth-quarter miracle.

> Timini: For right now, then, I'll just have to give you a giant THANK YOU.

———

The tacos might have given me superpowers.

As soon as Evie and I eat them, I get the idea to give the dress a more open back. We use some of the flowing fabric that goes over the chest and into the sleeves and continue it down along the deep V of the back of the dress. It turns out so much more beautiful than the original design had been.

And somehow, we get most of the costumes finished before the dozen castmates with the biggest parts show up for their fittings. Evie finishes up the last few ensemble costumes while I do the fittings, and everything works out. The actress playing Belle loves the dress so much she begs to wear it home.

Those superpowers from the tacos really are quite impressive.

Or maybe it's all Jackson, delivering food at a time when we couldn't function well any longer without it. Either way, I am grateful.

CHAPTER 10

Jackson

I DISCONNECT the conference call with the executive team and the international expansion team at Oliver Innovations, which includes both my parents and all three of my siblings as well as a handful of others, and shut my laptop. It's the beginning of their workday and the very end of mine on my last night in India.

During my three weeks here, I have not only managed to get a deal in the works for a manufacturing plant to start producing our mattresses and cushions, get contracts for distribution in the works, and get retailers on board to carry our product, but I've also made more connections than I ever imagined I'd be able to that will pave the way for future successes in this country.

By all accounts, everything about this trip has been more successful than I hoped for. Yet the thing that excites me the most at this moment is, strangely, not those successes. It's the fact that I will be able to meet Timini in person soon. I have never been so thrilled about a new relationship before. In fact, I've suspected I never would be. Yet here I am.

I grab all the shirts from the hotel's closet except for the one I will wear on the plane in the morning and start folding them, then drop each one into my suitcase.

Thinking back to every single person I've dated since college—or since high school, even—I am sure I haven't known any of them as well as I feel like I know Timini. Apparently, three weeks of nothing but talking has been rather effective. I can thank this trip for that. If I'd been home, I'd have given in and asked to see her in person a couple of weeks ago if being half a world apart hadn't stood in my way.

As effective as all the chatting has been in helping us to get to know each other, I am so glad that my flight leaves for home in the morning.

Over the past three weeks, we have discussed many things. Trivial things and soul-baring things. I have learned a lot about her, yet there is still so much I want to know. I've found out that she has a sister and several nieces and nephews. I've wanted to ask more, but I've been too worried that she will ask more about my family, and I haven't wanted to share that yet. Soon, though. Once we meet in person and have that connection outside of words typed on a screen, then we can cross that bridge. And that time is soon.

Now that meeting her in person is a very real and present thing, though, doubts and worries have started creeping in. Getting to know someone over a messaging app is one thing. Getting to know someone in person is entirely different. So much doesn't come through when it's just text. Will we connect the same way in person that we have through messages?

Timini does seem to genuinely like me. Will she still feel the same once she meets me in real life? And will everything still go as smoothly as it has been going?

My familiar habit of questioning the motives of anyone who seems to like me has popped up quite a few times, but I've mostly managed to push those away. The thing about having a lot of money and having an influential family is that it brings people close who are looking for something they think I can get them.

Which is fine. I don't mind helping people out in ways that I can. Except it means that I can never really trust whether the reason I seem to get along well with someone is because we are genuinely forming a friendship or if the person is just using me to get what they want.

But Timini doesn't know my last name. Or who my family is. Or who our company is. So I push those thoughts out whenever they surface. Well, I mostly do. Old fears and past relationships still try to haunt me, but I am aware of that fact, which helps. Still, though, money changes things. I have seen it up close and a little too personal in my life. I don't want it to touch my relationship with Timini.

I pick up my phone. It's getting late and I really need to pack, but it's only nine a.m. for Timini. I open the Chat Match app, tap on her name, and send her a good morning. After a couple of messages back and forth, I find out that she has already been working but has stopped for breakfast.

> Jackson: Do you have a breakfast food you eat every morning?

> Timini: Nope. It depends on how busy I am or how focused on a project I am. If I have tons of time, I'll always go for an omelet chock full of veggies. If I don't, then toast, a protein bar, an apple, or whatever is quick.

> Timini: I just remembered from your bio that you can't live without cold cereal and cartoons in the morning. Is there a specific cartoon or cereal?

> Jackson: Nope. That doesn't matter, as long as both are present.

It takes her a bit longer than normal to respond. I busy myself with packing so I won't feel quite as vulnerable and exposed.

> Timini: So the guy who is about the most responsible, self-disciplined, organized person I know eats breakfast like he's an eleven-year-old? Interesting. Tell me more.

I knew the question was coming—I set it up myself, after all. I just hadn't really thought through telling her. Maybe I brought up the question because I've wanted to share it with someone. Or maybe because I haven't exactly had my usual breakfast since I've been in India and I've missed the way it grounds me. I take a deep breath and then just spill all of it. The stuff I haven't told anyone before now.

Jackson: I feel like I had a strong sense of who I was when I was a kid. All through middle school and halfway through high school, even. Then I kind of lost sight of who I was for a while. Once I figured it out again, I started back with the daily cold cereal and cartoons of my childhood. It took me back to that time when everything was simple and I liked who I was. Even now, it still keeps me grounded.

It sounds stupid when I write it out like that. I wish I could take it back the moment I press send. But then her response comes in.

Timini: That's beautiful.

I wish I could see the expression on her face right now.

Timini: And it makes me want to toss this toast and boiled egg and eat Froot Loops.

Jackson: It might not give you superpowers, exactly, but who doesn't want to start off the day with a food whose box also includes such brain-stimulating games as "See how many Froot Loops you can stack on top of each other," and "Help Toucan Sam find his way through the maze."

Timini: Haha!

Timini: With as busy as my day is going to be today, I don't need brain stimulation as much as I need mental calmness. Tell me: what's the most relaxing situation you can imagine? Maybe it'll get me there.

Jackson: Being outside, preferably after sunset, walking in a slight rain.

Timini: Rain?! How can that be your most relaxing situation? A good half the time, the rain is freezing! You are no help at all.

Jackson: A slight freezing rain at night is the best time to go on a long walk. You live in Oregon but don't like the rain? How do you survive?

Timini: By soaking in the sunshine every chance I get.

Jackson: I forgot that you would prefer living in an oven. I'm going to call you Sunshine from now on.

Timini: You know it. Okay, it looks like I'm going to have to rely on my own most relaxing situation. It's on a beach with plenty of sunshine. Or in a canoe on a lake. Anywhere with a big body of water and a bright sun. Or even a skinnier body of water, like a rushing river. You're welcome to join me when you change your mind. ;)

Jackson: I'm not really a "body of water" kind of guy. I prefer it falling from the sky.

Timini: Like from a waterfall? Into a body of water?

> Jackson: Haha. Okay, I'm going to have to call you the winner of this conversation. And for now, I'll acquiesce on the body of water thing in the best interests of your need for brain relaxation.

Then I send her an animated gif of a sunny beach with the waves lapping at the sand.

> Jackson: Just to make sure we're still compatible, though, even with the body of water revelations… Let's say you go to Voodoo Doughnut. What kind do you choose?

> Timini: Apple Crumble, because it's like a pie in a doughnut. Plus: ginger snaps. Or the Portland Cream. You?

> Jackson: Solid choices there. I usually get Chuckles, because of the mix of chocolate, peanuts, and caramel, or the classic Bacon Maple Bar. Some days, though, it's more of a Grape Ape kind of day.

> Timini: A man who's got his priorities straight. Now I see why we matched.

I glance at my room, which currently looks like it could be declared a national disaster area. I really haven't made much progress since I disconnected from that conference call, and I have to be at the airport long before the sun rises.

Jackson: I'm traveling all day tomorrow, but I'll be home the day after. Want to meet for dinner?

I normally have no problem at all asking a woman out. Why does waiting for her answer make me feel like a nervous high school kid again?

Timini: I would love to.

I let out a huge breath of relief and start thinking of places where I can get a reservation this late and pull up a couple of restaurant's sites on my phone.

Jackson: How does Chef's Star at 7 sound?

Timini: Never been there. Sounds great! And so you'll recognize me when I come in, I have dark brown hair halfway down my back. Wavy. And there's a 99% chance I'll be wearing heels.

Timini: Who am I kidding? There's a 100% chance.

I smile and imagine how it's going to feel to finally see what she looks like. To be with her in person. My thumbs hover over my phone screen as I think about how to describe myself. Is there even anything about me I can mention that isn't average?

Jackson: I'll be wearing a dark gray suit with a light blue shirt.

Timini: I can't wait!

Nerves or not, neither can I.

CHAPTER 11
Timini

I RUN my hands down the length of my dress, smoothing everything out. Then I turn from one side to the other in the full-length mirror. Since Jackson said he's going to be wearing a suit and a light blue shirt, I decide I should wear a dress that goes with it. Mine is a deeper blue, bordering on navy, and is one of my favorites. The top is fitted yet still somewhat flowy, and the skirt ruffles above my knees just the right amount.

"You look beautiful!" Peyton says from where she, Bex, Addison, and Evie all sit on my unmade bed, watching me like I'm the most interesting TV show ever. "Do you think he's good-looking?"

I freeze. "I don't know. I mean, I assume so, but I guess I could be wrong." I realize that I have been picturing him based on how much I like chatting with him, and I have no idea if the guy in my head is anything like he is in real life.

Evie grins. "Here's hoping he's not a fifty-year-old couch potato."

A moment of panic hits before I remember that I already know his age—twenty-nine. And couch potatoes aren't the kind of people that companies send to put together huge business deals halfway around the world, or who get up at six a.m. to try to "match their high score" on getting ready for the day.

"I don't think I've ever seen you this nervous about a date before," Addison says.

I adjust my necklace and smooth my hair around my ear. "Well, I've never gone on a date with a guy I like this much before. Do I look too dressed up? I've never been to the restaurant, but he said he'll be wearing a suit."

"You look amazing," Evie says.

Bex nods. "You do. And I'm so proud of you for not self-sabotaging this time."

My attention whips to Bex. "What? I do not self-sabotage."

"You totally do. The whole time I've known you, you've always chosen guys where it's obvious that things won't work out, almost as if you're ensuring that things won't work out. But, from everything you've told us, Jackson sounds like a really good guy."

Peyton shoots Bex a look and then hops off my bed. She gives me a quick squeeze. "He does sound like a great guy. Now stop being nervous because this date is going to go better than hugs on a bunny."

I turn to look once more in the mirror. "Are you sure I look okay?"

"Yes!" all four women shout at the same time. So I take a deep breath and head down the stairs, all of them following close behind.

Both Ian and Roman are standing in the doorway to the family room, bonding over making it to the end of Thursday after rough work weeks while some kind of sporting event plays behind them on the TV. Both look over as I get to the lobby.

"Your Chat Match date, right?" Roman's smile is wide like a parent watching a kid learn to walk.

"Am I the first one to date someone from the app?"

He shakes his head. "We have a couple thousand people beta testing in the Portland area, so I doubt it. You're just the first one I know personally."

"Have fun," Ian says.

"And turn on your tracker!" Roman adds as I near the door.

I turn and give him a look.

"What? Do you know the guy's last name? Contact information?"

I don't. I actually haven't even thought about it since about the third day. I had been dying to ask him his last name so I could look him up on social media and get a glimpse of what he looked like. But then I thought about how I'd had a long line of poorly chosen dates based on looks, so I managed to convince myself that I most definitely didn't want that information. It would've just led to more bad choices.

"Safety first," Ian says and puts his arm around Addison as she snuggles up next to him.

Roman nods. "It's why we have the feature."

I take a deep breath and pointedly get out my phone, tapping the button that says I am going on a date with Jackson, where we are going to be, how long I anticipate us being there, and to automatically contact Peyton if I go somewhere unexpected. Then I hold up the phone as evidence that I did it.

Roman wears that smile again like he is so proud of his app that maybe his bad week was worth it. And I am glad—Jackson and I wouldn't have met if Roman hadn't decided to have his company make the app.

Thirty minutes later, I am still just as nervous as I pull up to the front of Chef's Star. I crane my neck, trying to see the parking lot, but I can't see it on either side of the building. I don't even notice that a man has been standing there in a valet's uniform until he steps forward. I roll down my passenger's window. "Could you direct me to the parking lot?"

"I'll take it for you."

I try to tell the man no thank you, that I can park and walk in just fine but he is already coming around to my side of the car. I let out a breath and look around. A few stray paper napkins are scattered around, a few random bags of things I meant to take into the inn, my running shoes lay on the floor in the back, and little fabric snips and strings are everywhere. Besides the fact that my little car is nowhere near fancy enough to be driven by a valet.

But he opens my door for me, so I grab my purse, pull the car's key off my key ring, and then hand it to the man. He gives me a ticket stub in exchange, and I thank him.

My nerves double and then triple as I walk up to the door. And then they shoot up exponentially when I walk into the lobby. I press a hand to my stomach. This place is way too expensive. I would've thought that Jackson knew me well enough to know that he didn't need to impress me by going to an expensive restaurant. But I really hope that is the reason why we are here—because he has a misguided need to impress and thinks a nice restaurant will do it, instead of places like this just being normal for him. It is probably because this is our first date. Maybe he is as nervous as I am to finally meet after getting to know each other so well. I step up to the host's table, a shiny polished mahogany, and tell him that I am meeting someone named Jackson.

He gives a quick nod. "Follow me, please."

The man leads me from the lobby, around a few dividers that look like light-covered trees growing up from the floor and disappearing into the ceiling, and into a cozy section of the restaurant. On the other side of the room, a man in a dark gray suit with a light blue shirt stands, and he is definitely a very fine man. Not a couch potato. Maybe a couch model. In fact, he could model anything—a gym membership, car repair tools, deodorant—and I would buy it whether I needed it or not.

I hope I am not blushing. I am probably blushing. So much heat has risen to my face that I must be. It's the Jackson blush I only get for him. And by the expression I am already able to make out on his face, he is looking at me much in the same way.

The man motions to the table as we near, says, "Your

waiter will be by shortly," and then turns and walks back to the lobby.

As I close the last few steps between us, things start looking familiar about the man. The way his eyebrows—thicker now than they were—seem to exist to perfectly frame his eyes. And those brown eyes have so much golden in them that they shine and make it feel like he can understand what I'm thinking without me saying a word.

The perfect dip just under his bottom lip that is now covered with a short scruff. Those ears that are the most symmetrical of anyone I've ever seen. The cheekbones that go up at the most perfect angle. The ones that were once soft and entirely kissable but are now strong and are still every bit as—

No! I am not thinking about planting kisses on those cheeks! I am furious that I am thinking of any nice things at all. This is the man who changed, after all. The man who got rich and broke my heart. And then stomped on it.

"Jack Oliver?" My words come out as a curse. A bomb whose explosion is barely contained.

His expression turns baffled. "Minnie?"

"*You're* who I've been chatting with?" A different kind of heat rises up in me. A kind that fills every last bit of me. I feel deceived by every traitorous feeling I've had while messaging him during the past three weeks.

"No wonder… Wow… I guess that makes…Wow." Jackson—or Jack, apparently—just keeps muttering in an awed voice.

I am not in awe. I am in shock. An angry, disbelieving, furious shock. A couple thousand people are beta-testing

Chat Match. Over three million people live in Portland and the surrounding areas. And I match with Jack Oliver.

The one guy I have connected with—the *only* guy I have connected with in years—and it has to be the one who so thoroughly broke my heart years ago.

I turn to walk away, but Jack reaches out and puts his hand on my arm. "Minnie. Timini. Wait."

I don't meet his eyes. I just shake my head. "This was a mistake." And then I stride out of the restaurant, my heels pounding on the ground with each step. I don't even slow down when my heel hits the floor a little harder than it is designed for and snaps right off. I just keep walking like my shoes are meant to be at two different heights, my right toes pointing up at the sky.

As the valet brings my car around, I glance at my broken, very recently adorable shoes. My luck with men is about as impressive as my luck with heels.

When I get back home and walk into the inn, I don't see a single one of my roommates, and Evie would've left long ago. Good—I'll have an unimpeded path up to my room. They must've all heard me get home, though, because within a minute, Addison, Bex, and Peyton have all made their way into my room. I unzip my dress, grab my fluffiest pajama bottoms and a tank top, and head into my bathroom to change.

When I come back out, I toss the dress over the back of my chair and point at Bex. "This was not self-sabotage. This was *the universe* coming together to sabotage *me*."

"What happened?" Peyton asks.

I pull my fancy barrette out of my updo, toss it on my

bed, and run my fingers through my hair in frustration. "It turns out that Jackson is Jack. My high school boyfriend."

"Oh," Bex says.

Addison looks from Peyton to Bex, then to me. "Isn't it sweet that you found each other after all this time? Wait. Why do you look like you want to stab something?"

I plop down on my bed and soon my roommates are all on the bed around me. I haven't told them much about Jack. It was so long ago that it hadn't seemed relevant. "I dated him all through my sophomore year in high school. He was a year older and he played a few different sports and he was so popular and I just felt so special that he liked me. Out of everyone.

"And he really was the sweetest boyfriend. *So* sweet. Whenever I had a rough day, he would slide a dozen notes telling me how awesome he thought I was into the slats at the top of my locker. Whenever things got crazy at home with my mom's boyfriend, he immediately planned something at his house that he wanted me to come to."

A chorus of "*Awws*" comes from my roommates.

"But his family owned a business. Oliver Innovations, actually."

Peyton's eyes open comically wide. "Wait. His last name is *Oliver*? He's one of those Olivers? The ones who make those beds with the stuff that's not memory foam or a gel but a squishy white stuff? I have one of those beds! And the shoe inserts. Oh my goodness."

"And I have their seat cushion on my office chair." Bex shakes her head. "I've actually met him. A couple of times.

Roman knows him, too. I can't believe you've been chatting with Jackson Oliver all this time!"

"Yeah, well, me neither." I am mad that I wasted so much time getting to know him. No… That isn't it at all. It isn't that I didn't enjoy our chatting. I am mad that I let my heart get invested when it was all just going to end and it was going to hurt.

"I'm sorry," Addison says. "I still don't get why this is a problem? I mean if he was a sweet boyfriend, and he's been great to chat with…"

"Because he didn't stay being that way!" I say. The emotions are strong and exhausting, and I turn to lie flat on my back. "I knew him all through middle school. We became friends my freshman year and started dating just before my sophomore year. Back in middle school, his family's business was small and struggling. Then, almost overnight in high school, it took off big time. And just as quickly, sweet Jack was gone and was replaced with a version who thought he was better than everyone. And I mean *everyone*. Seriously, I'd never met a more arrogant, entitled, awful jerk."

"And then he broke up with you?" Peyton asks.

I shake my head. "I mean, he probably would have, because he thought he was better than me, too. I was no longer good enough to even be in his house. And he definitely thought he was way too good to get anywhere near mine. But I beat him to the breakup. My heart was still just as broken either way. Mostly because of all that I had lost. I had known what it was like to date the amazing version of him."

For quite a while, all my roommates stay silent, and I just

play with the frayed edge of my favorite blanket, twisting it over and over in my fingers.

Then another thought emerges that I hadn't even realized I'd had until the words escape from my mouth in a whisper. "My mom went through a lot of boyfriends in my life up until that point, and every single one of them made her life worse. I loved Jack. He was supposed to be proof that it was only the guys my mom chose who were like that. Jack was supposed to show that love made things better. Instead, he proved that money ruins everything."

"You've gotten along pretty well now, though," Bex says. "Do you think you might be judging him solely off who he was twelve years ago?"

Peyton nods. "Does he feel like he's the same as he was back in high school?"

I let out a slow breath. "I don't know. People can put forth whatever persona they want to when all the communication is done over messaging."

"True," Addison says. "So how will you ever know if the guy you've been messaging with is like that if you don't get to know him in real life?"

I don't know. And I'm not sure I dare to find out.

CHAPTER 12

Jackson

I MAKE my way through the office, chatting with everyone extra after having been gone for so long. As happy as I am to be back, I just really want to get to my office before the delivery guy checks in..

I am still blown away that the Timini I've been talking to is Minnie. I've been wracking my brain ever since meeting for the dinner that didn't happen, trying to remember if I ever heard that her real name was Timini during any of the time I had known her in middle school and high school. I don't think I did.

But I desperately want to keep seeing her. I had been a world-class jerk back in high school when we broke up. Actually, I had been a jerk both before we broke up and after. My face burns just thinking about how I acted back then. I'm not sure I can convince her to take a chance on me again, but I am sure going to try.

I know she wouldn't appreciate flowers if I sent them to her—I remember that from when we were teens. But who knows? A lot has probably changed in the past twelve years. But I don't want to chance it. Instead, I go with my sister, Emma, to Voodoo Doughnuts and get all of her favorites plus a couple of mine. Then she helps me stick an eighteen-inch long small wooden dowel into each donut, and we arrange them in a vase like they're flowers. We even use tissue paper as the green stuff that is usually behind flowers.

I get a card and one of the plastic poker sticks that go in floral arrangements to hold it. On the card, I write out "I donut want things with us to end." It's cheesy, but it reminds me of the myriad of ways we had asked each other to school dances back in the day, and I hope it will make her smile.

And not at all remind her of the days when I had truly been a jerk to her.

Then I find a delivery driver who will take it to her place and is willing to contact me as soon as it has been delivered.

Emma sneaks into my office, seeming as if she's supposed to be in a meeting somewhere and is skipping so she can find out the results. I glance at the clock. In eleven minutes, I have to head to a meeting I can't skip. We both sit in silence, watching my phone—me trying not to bounce my leg incessantly and her trying not to bite her lip.

Finally, my phone lights up with a text from the delivery driver: *Just dropped it off. Thanks again for the big tip!*

I thank the man and then go back to staring at my phone.

"What now?" Emma asks.

I lift a shoulder in a shrug. "I know she's received them,

so it's not like I need to check in with her to see if they were delivered or anything like that. If she is willing to message me, she will. If she isn't, she won't." I try to act like it is no big deal, but it is a huge deal. I really like her and really want to get to know her in person again.

A full eight minutes go by. I finally convince myself to stop staring for a response that might never come in and am gathering my things for my meeting when my screen lights up. I nearly knock my phone off my desk in an attempt to grab it and swipe it open. Emma immediately jumps up and scoots in next to me so she can read, too.

> Timini: You were wise waiting until this morning to contact me.

> Timini: And you were wise to send donuts instead of flowers.

> Timini: The card was a nice touch.

> Jackson: Does this mean you'd be willing to meet in person again? I would love to talk face-to-face.

I hold my breath as I wait for her response.

> Timini: If I get to choose the place this time, and if it's tonight.

> Timini: Also, I'm not sure if I'm okay with this. No guarantee things with us will go past tonight.

> Jackson: Fair enough. Let me know the time and place, and I'll be there.

I put the phone on my desk, take a deep breath, and grin at my sister. "I got a second chance. I just have to make sure I impress her enough that she'll want more than that."

———

I pull into the parking lot of the Jumping Trolley in Gresham. I've never been to this particular Jumping Trolley, but Minnie and I went plenty of times to the one in Forest Grove when we were in high school. It was one of the few places to hang out that was both cool and inexpensive enough for our teenage wallets.

I smile. It could not be a more different place than the restaurant where I tried to have dinner with her last night. It is loud, not intimate. Cheap, not elegant. Passable food, not award-winning. Just like the one in Forest Grove, a cover band of forty-somethings plays on the raised stage on the weekends. I suspect we aren't here because of the nostalgia or even because it's a place that Timini likes. The reason we are here is precisely because it is the opposite of where I picked. She is trying to see how I will do outside of what she thinks is my element.

Chef's Star is definitely in my element. But so is Jumping Trolley. Mostly.

As soon as I walk into the restaurant, my eyes immediately find Timini. She is sitting at a table toward the side of the room, but not in a booth, and she takes my breath away. Her smile is bright even if it does have a hint of trepidation behind it. Her hair is loose and curly, and she is wearing jeans and heels, and that is now my favorite combination of clothing items ever.

As I walk over to her, a strange buzzing fills my insides. I don't know what it is, exactly—all I know is that I am so glad that she agreed to see me again.

"Is this okay?" she asks as I near.

I grin and take the other seat at the table. I want to say that I would've gone anywhere, even if it had been to get hot dogs from that one convenience store we went to that one time when we both got food poisoning. That would've been too much, though. Instead, I say, "It's great."

We order our food, and just like when we were teens, Timini orders dessert along with her meal, so I do, too. As we get our food and start eating, our small talk is awkward and stilted. Not at all easy, like our conversations over the app have been.

But it does give me a chance to fully take her in and see how much she has changed since we were teens. She has the same mischievous gleam in her fiercely blue eyes. Those long lashes still frame them just as beautifully. They contain a strength that is new, but they have that warmth that I've always loved.

Her face is still as stunning and is even more refined. It is as if the last dozen years have taken everything amazing about her and made it impossibly better. I can't take enough of it in, no matter how long I sit across from her.

When she purses her lips just on one side, it reminds me of every time she did exactly that when we were teens and she was thinking through something.

I set my napkin on the table. "I think it's time to address

the elephant in the room. I was not a good person at the end of my junior year and that summer before I moved. Actually, I was still not a good person for a bit longer than that. And I definitely didn't treat you the way I should've treated you. That is a part of my life that I'm not proud of, and I hope that I'm nothing like the guy I was back then. I should've found out where you lived a long time ago and apologized for everything, and I'm very sorry I didn't."

She picks up a fry and eats it, studying me as she chews. Then she gets a forkful of her layered chocolate cake and pauses right before the bite reaches her mouth. "And you're sorry about standing me up for that date when you went and hung out with your friends? And then took a page out of my mom's boyfriend's playbook and made me feel like I was overreacting when I brought up the fact that you hadn't even let me know? Or about humiliating me in front of both my friends and yours?"

My face burns with shame and embarrassment. "I'm especially sorry about that." That hadn't been the worst of it, either. Thoughts of how I acted back then feel like a brick in my stomach.

She eats her bite of cake, so I take a bite of my cheesecake, too. Mostly because it makes things slightly less awkward and not at all because my stomach wants me to add anything to the brick that's already there.

Timini reaches a hand out and places it on my forearm. My eyes are immediately drawn to it and the electricity that buzzes through me at her touch. When my eyes go to hers, she says, "I forgive you."

I had no idea how badly I needed to hear that until she

says it. I exhale, and my whole body seems to fill with light, making my heart feel like it is floating, my throat feeling like it is closing off. I swallow hard. My eyebrows draw together, and I look down at my cheesecake. "Was that almond extract?" I ask, my voice scratchy.

"Oh! You're allergic, aren't you?"

I'm not epi-pen allergic. I'm just uncomfortable-squeezing allergic. Raspy-voice allergic. That is all. Nothing catastrophic. "I'll be fine. I just…" I stand up. "Give me a minute."

I hurry toward the restroom on the opposite side of the building. Once inside, I turn on the cold water and splash some on my face. Then I splash some more, hoping it'll somehow mimic going outside on a chilly night. It isn't, exactly, but it helps a little. I lean in close to the mirror to see how awful I look and immediately jerk back when I realize I've leaned against a very wet counter, soaking my shirt.

Great. That is just what I need—a shirt that now looks like I don't know how to make it through an uncared-for restroom unscathed. I turn to grab paper towels for my face, my hands, and my shirt, but the dispenser is empty.

Of course, it is.

I shake off my hands, wipe them on my pants, and then pull my shirt up enough to wipe off my face. Not that it needs any more water on it. Then I head out to the restaurant to find someone who can give me some paper towels.

I go to a little alcove where the wait staff works, tell them about the restroom, and they say they will get some paper towels for me. Sounds of cheering grab my attention, so I look as the lead singer makes his way down into the audience, chatting and making jokes with the people sitting at the nearest tables, looking for someone to come up on stage with him.

My eyes immediately go to Timini. She is easily the most beautiful woman in the room, and she is sitting all alone— there is no way the lead singer isn't going to ask her to go up on stage. I don't know if she'd like that or not. I turn to the waitress in the alcove and ask if I can just grab a couple of napkins from her so I can head back to Timini more quickly.

As soon as they are in my hand, I turn and nearly knock into the lead singer of the band.

"You look like someone who's ready to perform," the man says, his band playing a repeating tune from the stage. "What's your name?"

"Um, Jackson." My voice is still just as scratchy as it was when I first took the bite of cheesecake. I can breathe okay enough to get by, but I won't be running anytime in the next few minutes.

"Patrick up there needs to take a song off. Why don't you come up on stage and be our backup singer for one?"

I shake my head. "I can't sing." Forget the allergic reaction—I can't on a good day.

The man—a guy with a goatee, fancy jeans, and graying hair by his temples—leans in close and whispers like he's trying to tell me a secret, except he's whispering into the microphone for all to hear. "Want to know a secret? It doesn't matter if you can or not, as long as you do it with enough confidence."

I glance at Timini. She's watching me, a curious, inter- ested expression on her face.

Then, one of the guys up on stage—Patrick, probably— starts chanting into his microphone, "Go on stage, go on stage," and within seconds, everyone in the restaurant is chanting the same.

What am I supposed to do—tell him no? If Timini chose this location as a test to see if I can feel as comfortable in a place like this as I used to be, I think saying no would mean failing that test. So I do like the man suggests. I walk up to the front of the room and get on stage with as much confidence as a guy can whose throat is closed off and whose shirt is soaked, clearly from a poor choice at the bathroom sink. The man hands me a tambourine, of all instruments, and clips a mic to my shirt.

Then the band starts playing "Livin' On a Prayer" by Bon Jovi, which I'm grateful for. My scratchy voice matches that much better than it would have with a song from, say, Mariah Carey. I bang the tambourine against my hand until the chorus comes along. Then I take a deep breath and sing, my voice rough and ragged from my current situation, and also so very off-tune from my all-the-time situation.

Eventually, I manage to stop caring what I look and sound like, which is rather impressive considering how very badly I want to impress Timini. But I'm pretty sure that impressing her definitely dropped off the menu a while ago.

When the song finally ends, I bow to the applause, then jump off the stage and walk back to the table where Timini is clapping along with the rest of the room. She stands to greet me and moves in so close that I can feel her warmth and smell her citrus perfume. My senses are on high alert, trying to catch it all.

Then she leans in even closer, bringing her lips near to my ear. Her breath tickles my skin, sending waves of voltage plowing through me. I don't know if she's going to kiss my cheek or tell me I did a good job or something I haven't even imagined yet, but I'm going crazy waiting to find out.

Then she whispers, ever so gently into my ear, "Your fly is down."

I close my eyes, trying to block out everything in this entire building as I sit down and attempt to surreptitiously zip my pants.

Maybe this date was doomed from the start. As our waitress passes by, I ask for the check. I just need to pay and get out of here as soon as possible. Then Timini and I can each drive our separate ways, and I can start working on what is sure to be a very long, painful process of forgetting that this night ever happened.

Timini puts her elbow on the table, her chin resting in her palm, studying me. I'm not even sure what happened to the napkins the waitress handed me before I went up on stage, but for a moment, I think about using my napkin at the table on my shirt. Then I decide that it doesn't really matter at this point.

I meet Timini's eyes again. Mostly because hers haven't left mine, and it's awkward to keep avoiding them.

But then the waitress sets down the check, the spine of its folder ripped so far up that it barely holds together. I slip in cash to cover the bill and a tip good enough to make the teenage waitress's night and hand it back.

When we head outside, I walk Timini to her car. Instead of getting in and driving away as fast as she can, like I've assumed she will, she leans against it, studying me again. Finally, she speaks. "I think we should go out again."

"I…what?" There is no way I heard that correctly.

"You aren't the same guy you were just before you moved. Tonight, you weren't protecting your image or your ego—you were thinking about people. Tonight, I saw the man I've been chatting with for weeks, not the teenager who broke my heart."

That's what she got out of this night? I no longer care about all the things that went wrong if it brought her to that conclusion.

She takes a step closer to me, her eyes flicking from mine to my lips and back to my eyes. She's back. We're back. We're suddenly back to the point we'd been when it was all just messages sent over a dating app.

Except now, I'm seeing her in person. Talking to her. Feeling her hand as she places it on my chest, right over my heart. Fireworks and cannons erupt in me, and I reach out and cradle the side of her face with one hand and wrap the other around her waist. She immediately closes the remaining space between us, and I press my lips to hers.

I know my lips are moving with hers to fill a desperate need to have her in my life. To fill a longing for her that I hadn't known was so strong until this moment. Then she lets out a small moan that tells me that maybe she wants this relationship to work out just as desperately as I do.

And that makes my whole body relax into the kiss. I soak in the softness of her lips, the warmth of her breath, and the smoothness of her cheek as I run my thumb along it. Then I bring my other hand up to cup her face as well, feeling like

I'm holding something precious. Beyond worth. I break the kiss and rest my forehead against hers as we both breathe heavily.

"Woah," she breathes. "And I thought you were a good kisser back in high school. But that… Wow. That was incredible."

I have to agree—she definitely is incredible.

CHAPTER 13
Timini

I **LOOK** up from the suit coat I'm sewing when my older neighbors, Carol and Meera, walk into the dining room. Peyton hurries out from behind the kitchen island, where she's cooking food for a client, to give the women hugs, and my assistant, Evie, waves at them.

"Thank you for being willing to do this," Meera says as she hands me a skirt. "Normally, I would ask Shirley for help, but since she's off visiting her newest great-grandchild, I had to go to Carol, and…let's just say that wearing it unfixed would've been better."

Carol shrugs. "In my defense, I warned her about my lack of skill before I touched it."

"Well, I figured you'd at least be better at it than me!" Meera turns to me. "And I haven't sewn a stitch in my life. Are you sure you have time to fix it?"

"Yep," I say, moving some of the items from one of the round tables to another so I can spread the skirt out to see what it needs, "because I have Evie. She has kept us on track and aimed in the right direction. We just met with the directors of both shows yesterday, and they both approved the direction we are going with all of the pieces. We even did an impromptu fitting with a couple of the actors who were in the building. We should have no problem meeting our deadline in two weeks. Oh wow, what happened here?"

It looks like the skirt had ripped at the seam. But instead of turning it inside out and sewing the seam so the raw edges would be on the inside of the garment, it appears that Carol placed the two sides one on top of another and then just stitched across it all. And it's not even a straight line.

Carol shrugs, palms up. "Hey, I never said I was an expert."

I grab my seam ripper and go to work undoing the stitching.

"So," Meera says, "how are things with your new man?"

I miss a stitch and poke the end of the seam ripper into the fabric. Luckily, I wasn't pressing hard enough to do any damage. But the question apparently has the ability to make my mind stop working as it simultaneously turns me to goo.

"Addison told us that he's your ex," Carol says.

I smile and go back to work, focusing more this time. "Yeah, and that made it really awkward for a bit, but we got past it. Things are actually going pretty great."

More than great, actually. We've seen each other nearly every night for the past couple of weeks, and we've been texting during the day, too. I've been surprised to find out that he's like the version of Jack I dated in high school before he turned into a jerk, not the guy he became after. Except he's had twelve years to become even more incredible. I never thought I'd enjoy dating someone so much.

"They're adorable together, too," Evie says as I finish removing Carol's stitching and take it to my sewing machine. "He knows that Timini thinks things are going to turn out well if she sees the number one in random places. Well, Jackson's company's offices are in Portland, and they just happen to be pretty close to Hamilton Hall. So yesterday, he snuck over there before our meeting with the directors, guessed where we would likely park, and placed a bunch of sticky notes with the number one written on them in random places all along our path from there to the front door."

A smile spreads across my face just thinking of it. I snip off the stray strings on the part I've sewn, then turn around to my serger to reinforce the seam and keep it from fraying.

"He's come over for a couple of roommate dinners," Peyton says to the sound of chopping vegetables. "You should see the two of them together. It makes you feel like you're wrapped in a warm, fuzzy blanket. I made lasagna and homemade breadsticks for dinner last time. Everyone was already seated when I took them out of the oven. As I brought it to the table, everyone's eyes were on the food with that look you get when you're really excited about what you're about to eat and just can't wait until it's right there in front of you. Except Jackson. He still had that same look on his face but his eyes were on Timini, not on the food."

Carol whips around to face me, pointing a bent finger at me. "You marry that man!"

I laugh. I'm not actually looking to get married, but I do love Carol's enthusiasm.

"Aww," Evie says, "I want a boyfriend like that."

"Are you single?" Carol asks. "Because I have a grandson."

Evie lifts the presser foot on her sewing machine and pulls out the piece she's working on, snipping the threads. "No, I have a boyfriend. He's just…not like that."

"Well," Meera says, "maybe it's time you dropped him like a wad of cash at Costco and get yourself someone who is." Evie nods, but even Meera picks up on the fact that Evie's expression says she doesn't want to keep discussing her love life. So she turns to Peyton. "And what about you? How much longer do you have until you tie the knot?"

Peyton sighs happily. "Thirteen days. In less than two weeks, I'll be Peyton Peyton and I'll get to wake up every morning next to Max."

We all sigh just as happily. Really, it's hard not to when it's Peyton. She just makes everything seem heavenly. At least I don't have to stress about who to take to the small event. Jackson has already agreed to join me.

"Then Max is going to move in here until Bex's new house is finished and she and Roman move out. Then we'll get our own place. So we'll be here for about three and a half months."

"It's five now," I say. "The builder ran into more problems."

"Aw, poor Bex and Roman!" Peyton makes a sad face, and then it instantly goes back to happy. "But hey, more time with all of us together!"

"Ask Meera why she's so interested in everyone's love life," Carol says.

Meera wears an expression that is much too innocent-looking to actually be innocent. "What? I'm just interested in our neighbors. I'm being neighborly."

Carol crosses her arms and raises an eyebrow. "Okay, then, ask her what she needs the skirt for." When Meera doesn't respond quickly enough, she says, "She's going dancing with a boy tonight!"

Peyton, Evie, and I all cheer and whoop while Meera blushes. Then she playfully slaps Carol's shoulder. "My goodness. With *a boy*. You make it sound like I'm in eighth grade again. I won't ever get over my Faris, but some companionship would be nice. Jerry is a widower, and he's been asking me to go dancing with him for weeks. I woke up one day and went, 'Do you know what? I want to go dancing.'"

"We should celebrate," I say as I toss the repaired skirt to Meera. Then I hurry out of the kitchen and head across the lobby to the big family room. Bex is working on something on her laptop that she seems pretty focused on but Bex is always up for a distraction. "Want to join us for an impromptu dance party?"

Bex immediately perks up, grabs her phone, and starts scrolling through something. Music, probably.

"Is Addison home?"

Bex looks up from her phone. "She came home to get some organizational supplies for a client, and I don't think I've heard her come back down."

I go to the base of the stairs and yell up, "Addison! Dance party in the kitchen!"

Addison comes bounding down the stairs just as Bex's

phone connects with the inn's speakers, and dance music floods the inn.

The three of us join Peyton, Evie, Carol, and Meera in the kitchen, and we all dance to the music, not caring how uncoordinated any of us look, weaving in and out of the six small tables that are covered in fabric, costumes, machines, notions, and patterns. Impromptu dance parties are what get me through any challenge, and I love that my roommates feel the same way about them.

None of the guys are home, but Ian, Roman, and Max have all joined in before. We haven't done an impromptu dance party with Jackson around, so I don't know how he would react to knowing how much of a necessity they are. But the man got up on stage to play the tambourine and be a backup singer when he had a water mishap in the bathroom and a voice that could barely squeak out words. My guess is he would join in.

I'm surprised at how much I want him to be around all the time just so he'll happen to be here for the next one.

My phone blares, even louder than the music, and I find it under a folded costume. I look at the number on the screen and then answer the call. "Hi, Mom." I press my hand against my other ear and head out to the front porch so I can hear her above the music.

"Hi, Minnie."

Two short words, and I can already hear the stress in her voice.

"Is everything okay?"

"You said you were going to come help me organize the storage room yesterday, but then you never came."

"Oh! Mom, I'm sorry—I completely forgot about that." Maybe I should see if Evie would be willing to organize my personal schedule as masterfully as she organizes my work one. "Why didn't you call me when I didn't show up?"

"I figured you had more important things to do than to help me. Keala, too. I wasn't going to call at all, but it's too big of a job for me, and Neal just keeps complaining about it, and—"

Whenever my mom gets a new boyfriend, it always starts off with euphoria. Then, as their relationship gets more serious, each one makes her react a little differently, and always in a bad way. This one makes her stressed out and unsure of people's motivations. I don't know the guy super well; he had only dated my mom for a couple of weeks before he moved in, and that was only a month ago.

"Mom. I don't mind helping. I just got focused on something and forgot." I can't even remember what stole my focus at the time I was supposed to leave. Maybe a project. Or the Hallmark movie I convinced Jackson to watch with me. Or anything, really. Forgetting things is too often a state of being for me. "Can I come tonight instead?"

"Yes," she squeaks out.

"I'll be there. Mom?"

"Yeah?"

"We'll get it done tonight. No worries."

She lets out a long breath and then takes in a few slow breaths. Her next words come out calmer. "Okay. Thanks, kiddo."

I disconnect the call and then call my sister, Keala. Her two older kids are in school but the chaos of the younger three can still be heard. "We forgot to go help Mom organize her storage room last night."

"Oh, shoot! Is she a ball of stress?"

"You know it."

Keala lets out a long sigh. "I really can't wait until she breaks up with this one."

"Me neither."

I make plans with my sister to help that night and then hang up just in time to see a text from Jackson pop up. It's a picture he has sneakily taken while in a meeting that shows nothing, really, except part of one of his legs and one foot, saying he is thinking of me, and it makes my heart beat double-time.

Like euphoria.

A pang of worry stabs me in my heart. But then I push it away. I am not going to let my relationship with Jackson turn out like every single one of my mom's relationships always do.

CHAPTER 14

Jackson

I KNOW that Timini's day has been busy, but she somehow still looks amazing when I pick her up. Her hair is in a low, loose bun at the nape of her neck, with pieces of hair that haven't stayed in the bun curling by her face and neck. One part, in particular, touches her neck right at the spot where it curves into her shoulder, and all I can think of is how much I want to kiss that spot.

Something seems off, though, and I can't quite tell what it is. Maybe I can get her to say what it is if I ask the right questions. "How did things go at your mom's last night?"

Her brows pull together for a quick second like my question is so far from what is on her mind that it takes a moment for her to pull back. "It went great. It actually wasn't as huge of a job as my mom had imagined it was, and with all three of us working together and having fun doing it, we were finished in no time."

So it's not that, then. I glance over again as I stop at a

traffic light before getting on the interstate. She runs her hands down the fitted skirt she's wearing and then looks out the window at nothing in particular.

"Oh!" I say. "You're nervous about tonight. Why are you nervous?"

She looks over at me, and I take a glance back at her before I pull the car forward and maneuver into the lane that will merge onto the freeway.

"Oh, I'm just meeting your family tonight, along with your business friends. Why would you think I'd be nervous?"

I reach out, find her hand, and give it a squeeze. "Okay, first off, it's just my family. You've already met them. They're not scary."

"It's been twelve years since I've seen them, Jackson. It's not like I know them anymore. A lot has changed since I saw them last."

"Fair enough. But they like you."

"Not Naomi. She's never liked me."

"Naomi's just intense. People think she doesn't like them all the time, but I swear that's just her thinking face. And she thinks a lot. Besides, she'll be in a good mood because we're going to be having cake for her birthday."

"It's her birthday, and you didn't tell me?" Timini sounds even more stressed than she was before.

"It's not a big deal. It's not a big birthday celebration or anything. I went with my parents and siblings to her house last night to give her presents while you were at your mom's. Her building doesn't allow candles, though—long story—so we are just blowing out the candles tonight. That's all. I promise it will be fine.

"And as far as the business thing after, it's just a small reception. Not more than a dozen people. And since it's at my parents' house, you'll basically have the home-field advantage by that point. Not a big deal at all."

For the rest of the drive from Quicksand to my parents' place in Lake Oswego, I banter with Timini, like we do over text and over the app's message system while I was in Delhi. I think it's really helped her nerves to relax.

When we get to my parents' front door, before I open it, I turn to her and cup her face in my hands. I give her a look that I hope will make the feeling that everything will be okay sink into her. She smiles up at me, and I just want to drink every bit of her in. And then I kiss those beautiful lips of hers. She melts into me, so she must've gotten the message.

She seems content to stay outside, kissing, all night long. And I'm tempted to do just that. But my family is just on the other side of the door, so I finally pull my lips away. "Come on. I want you to meet my family."

My mom welcomes Timini the moment we walk through the door, complimenting her and trying to make her feel at home. My dad is right behind her, introducing himself. Naomi, Ethan, and Emma are already here, and none of them have brought dates. I introduce them all, and they are kind and welcoming, too. Emma even manages to keep her excitement that Timini is here from bursting over too much. We make our way past the foyer and into the family room.

"Your home is beautiful," Timini tells my mom.

She thanks Timini, but I look at her curiously. There's

something behind the words that I can't quite guess. Not enough for my mom to notice, but I've known her well enough to see it hiding.

The more I try to figure it out, the more I realize that she is uncomfortable—she's just very good at hiding it. I look around at the large family room through her eyes. The vaulted ceilings, the ornate trim, the nice furniture, the family picture over the mantel, the art on the walls, the big dining room and kitchen off to the side, and the patio that can be seen beyond the floor-to-ceiling windows. I love my parents' house. It's nice, but also feels warm and homey. I can't guess what about it is making her uncomfortable.

We all chat, and Timini seems to get along with my family so well. I haven't realized how much I've yearned for this until I feel the weight of it lift from my shoulders.

"Well," my mom says, putting her hands on her knees, "we are going to have guests showing up in thirty minutes or less, so we better get to lighting those candles!"

I offer a hand to Timini and pull her to standing. For a moment, we are only inches apart, and she leans into me and whispers, "I like your family. They're more down-to-earth than I was expecting."

I put a hand on the small of her back, guiding her to the dining room table, grinning the whole time. I pull out a chair for Timini and then sit down next to her, and Naomi takes a seat on the opposite side of the table, across from me. She keeps giving Timini odd looks like she wants to say something, but she never does.

Ethan cuts the cake and puts it onto plates, and Emma practically skips around the table as she puts one in each spot. Then my mom follows behind Emma, putting a candle in each person's piece.

Timini's forehead crinkles. "You do candles in everyone's cake?"

I'm surprised to realize I never had her over for a family birthday celebration in high school.

"You can thank me for that," Ethan says before licking the frosting off the knife and setting it aside.

My mom smiles at Timini. "Since Ethan and Emma are twins, they both had candles in their cakes. When Ethan was little, he couldn't understand why everyone wouldn't have candles if they did, so we just went with it. Once he was old enough to understand, he said that since they were the only ones getting presents, everyone else should at least get wishes. It spilled over into everyone's birthdays, and it just kind of became a tradition."

"That's sweet," Timini says. "I like it."

My dad goes around the table and lights each candle. He only has two left when Naomi bursts out, "I'm sorry I hated you in high school!"

My eyes fly to my sister as Timini tenses beside me. *Everyone* seems to be frozen in place, actually. Timini was right about Naomi not liking her? And why hadn't Naomi liked her? Naomi looks embarrassed. And then, like she has been holding her evidence in for far too long, it all seems to spill out of her in a rush.

"Even though we were in the same grade, I hadn't known you too well before you started dating Jackson. And then we were in a history class together. The teacher split us into groups and each group was supposed to make a diorama of a Revolutionary Era town. I was a group leader and you were, too, remember?

"Anyway, I practically had to bribe my group to meet together, and even so, I only got them to come over three times, so I had to do hours and hours of work on it by myself. And then in class, Mr. Zabinski reminded us that it was due in two days and I saw the look on your face—you had completely forgotten about it. So I thought your group's was going to be awful. Especially because after class, you gathered your group together and said to bring ideas and supplies the next day and you were just going to meet at a table in the lunchroom and put it together during lunch.

"And then I watched you guys do it the next day and there was no organizing of the ideas—everyone just started making things and throwing them in and I knew my group's was going to be the best, especially since we spent so much more time on it, but then your group's was the crowd favorite. So, I'm sorry I was mad about that.

"And then you broke up with Jackson. And I know he was being an"—her eyes shoot to our mom for a second—"sorry, Mom—a pack mule's hind end, but I would hear him crying about it at night in his room when he didn't think anyone could hear. And that just really made me not like you even more. And then we moved away for that year, and I didn't really see you when we moved back. And then I just kind of forgot all about you. Anyway, you're actually very lovely. Jackson has told us so many great things about you, and you're everything he said, and it just makes me feel even worse for not liking you back then. Will you forgive me?"

Naomi reaches a hand across the table toward Timini. I am in shock at all my sister has just spilled, and I don't manage to take my eyes off her until I see movement out of the corner of my eye and turn to see Timini reaching out for Naomi's hand.

"I forgive you."

Our table is wide, though, so she really has to stretch to reach Naomi's hand.

And that's when I smell burning hair, and everyone lets out some kind of sound between a startled shriek and a guttural shout as Timini jerks back. I'm not sure who starts smacking at her hair to get it to stop burning first. All I know is that one of our hands manages to catch her plate on the way to her hair, and it lands with the frosting side of the cake pressed into her shirt.

Everyone in the room freezes in stunned silence, our eyes on the lock of hair that apparently burnt through right in the middle because a perfect curl lies on the table. The perfect curl that had rested on the curved part of Timini's neck earlier—the spot I'd wanted to kiss.

Timini tries to peel the cake off her shirt. Half of the frosting stays put and the other half, including the candle, is still stuck to the smashed piece. Big crumbles of it fall to the table as she puts it back on the plate.

"Please tell me you at least made a wish before that candle went out," Ethan says, picking up his fork.

My shock only grows that my brother would joke about that.

But then Timini lets out a sound that is a mix between an

exhale and a laugh. "I did—I wished that I'd make tonight more memorable."

And just like that, the tension in the room deflates and everyone starts chuckling. How quickly Timini can recover from something like that and how easily she forgives is astounding to me. I can tell that she's holding some tension that she is trying to keep hidden, though.

"Come on," my mom tells her. "Let's get you in a new blouse."

Timini throws her a grateful look and then gives me a smile and a shoulder squeeze before getting up and leaving the room with my mom.

"I like her," Emma says before taking a bite of her cake.

My dad turns to me. "Listen, son. I know you're not going to like this, but I just got a message and wanted to warn you. Remember how we invited Robin to the get-together tonight?"

I nod. Her family owns a company that we partner with on a few things, so we make sure to keep things cordial with them. My attention is still on Timini's retreating back, though. I am warring between following her to see if there is anything I can do and forcing myself to stay in my seat because helping right now would probably be the opposite of helpful.

"She is dating someone new, and she's bringing him tonight."

I don't get why my dad thinks I'd have a problem with that. Robin isn't someone I've ever wanted to date. The fact that she is dating someone is great news.

When I don't react, my dad continues. "The guy she's dating is Harper."

Oh.

Harper and I were actually good friends. Or, at least, I thought we were. I hadn't found out that the guy had been using me and hadn't had any interest in actually being friends until a year later when he used some sensitive company information he got from me to buy his way into a position at a rival company.

The betrayal hurt Oliver Innovations. Probably not as badly as Harper thought it would, but I am still feeling the damage the guy did to me personally. His betrayal made me question the motives of everyone who wanted to get close to me a good ten times more than I had before. And now I am going to have to spend the evening in the same room with the guy.

I meet my dad's eyes. "I thought we agreed that Harper was never going to step foot in this house again."

"And he doesn't have to," my dad says. "Robin didn't send the email until they were almost here, but I can email back and say they aren't welcome. Or, I can stand at the door, tell them to leave, and physically stop him from coming in."

I shake my head. That would damage relations with Robin and her company, and I don't want that. "No, it's okay. I can handle Harper for one night."

I take a deep breath. At least I'll have Timini by my side. I can get through this.

CHAPTER 15
Timini

THERE'S a reason all the kids in school called me "Mini." I was petite back then, and not much has changed.

Mrs. Oliver, however, is not. She's plenty thin, but she's also tall and graceful and could pretty much walk around with a crown and the title of "Empress" and no one would question it.

So, grateful as I am that Jackson's mom has taken pity on me and has brought me to her own closet (which is big enough to park my car in) to help me out, wearing one of Jaclyn Oliver's blouses makes me feel like a kid playing dress-up.

I walk down the winding staircase into the family room and Jackson's eyes find mine immediately, a tentative smile on his face. Good golly, he is one beautiful man. How did I ever think I could stay away when I first found out he was Jack in that restaurant? I return his smile and take his proffered hand in mine.

"Is everything okay?"

"Totally. It's cool to have your boyfriend's mom dress you so you'll look good at their business event."

He grimaces.

"Really, though, I'm super grateful. I would much rather be wearing this than a cake-and-frosting-covered blouse."

The doorbell rings and Emma says, "I'll be on door duty!" and practically skips her way to the door. I draw in a slow, deep breath and try to get the Zumba party in my stomach to calm down as Jackson turns to greet the first of the night's guests.

Something I learn very quickly is that business people are on time. That, or they all arrive on a bus together. I'm guessing it's the former, though, because I really can't picture them all on a bus together. All I know is that "a dozen people" means "a dozen plus dates, if they brought someone, so more like twenty." Twenty people—plus Jackson's family—to make small talk with, memorize the names of, and try not to embarrass myself in front of.

I remind myself that I'm here, in Jackson's family room, milling around with a couple dozen people because it means a lot to Jackson. And because "you can't experience new lands from the confines of your comfort zone" and all that. But this is so far out of my comfort zone that I need a map.

Sure, I run my own business, and I'm in a room full of business people. But these aren't people like my roommates, who I met at the Creative Women Entrepreneurs seminar. These are people who help run big, multinational corporations, and I don't think I could feel more out of place.

Well, actually, I do feel more out of place than just that. I sneak a hand up and tuck the lock of hair that is now only an inch and a half long into the part that is pulled back. Jaclyn got me a pair of scissors to trim the singed ends, but that lock doesn't exactly look natural or like it's meant to be that short.

Then I adjust my shirt again. Not that I need to—the thing goes halfway to my knees. Why didn't I ask for a scarf to tie around my waist? Or simply tucked it in?

I can do this. Jackson leads me to a group of three people who are talking and introduces me to them. I've learned that I can remember people's names more easily if I tie them with something else as soon as I hear it. So when Jackson introduces me to a guy named "Drew," I think of the word drew, like he drew a picture. I imagine him drawing a picture and me getting out a big black marker and writing his name on his breast pocket.

Which is great, except before I even finished tying Drew's name to him, I had two more names thrown at me in quick succession, followed just as quickly by a need to follow the conversation. And the small talk for this group is always about business, never about the weather or how the Trail Blazers are going to play this year. We aren't even two minutes into the conversation when I have to use the guy's name and call him Mark. *Mark.* Because my brain somehow remembers that I marked his name on his shirt, not drew it on.

At the guy's expression, which hovers somewhere between confused and offended, I try to explain that it's because the two names are similar and I wrote it down wrong. When his expression drops "offended," keeps "confused," and adds "judging my lack of an IQ," I stop talking. With how this night is going, I would probably prove him right if I continued.

This place is making me itchy. Everything about this home is rich and elegant and everything I've learned to dislike about money. So are all the people in the room. I've had enough experience around rich people to know that they are not super likely to be nice people regardless of how nice they are acting.

I like dressing up and looking nice. But that is only part of who I am. Being here makes me feel like I'm a messy bun and yoga pants kind of girl in a coiffed hair and pencil skirt world.

I make it through meeting and chatting with the next half dozen people without an incident. I put little check marks in my head for each one because they make me feel rather accomplished right now.

As Jackson leads me across the room toward some other people he wants to socialize with, he puts an arm around my waist and I tuck myself into his side, loving the small moment to just soak him in. I turn my face to him. "You've got a lot of friends here. They're nice, and they seem to really love you."

There's an uncomfortable look on Jackson's face, and I think I know why. "Well, except for that one guy. Harper, right? He tries to come across as a good guy but he's not."

Jackson stops our path toward a small group of our guests and gives me a curious look. After a pause, he says, "Then you are better at sensing authenticity than I am. It took me a year of becoming really good friends with him before I figured that out. If I'd had your help back then, it would've saved me a sizeable number of struggles."

I look at him, hoping he will tell me more. He lets out a quick breath. "Let's just say that the experience left me questioning everyone's motives and wondering what they were looking to gain."

So that was the source of the uncomfortable look I saw on his face when I said that people here loved him. How does he manage to enjoy this world? It seems like he feels the same way about it that I do.

He looks away at a random spot on the wall and says in a low voice, like he's embarrassed to admit it, "It has just left me wondering if people only like me for outside reasons."

I reach a hand up and turn his face toward mine, then place my hand on his chest. "I like you for inside reasons."

The smile he gives me is wide and beautiful and very genuine. And it makes me want to just stare at his face all night. Well, except for the times when I'm kissing those beautiful lips of his.

But preferably not in this place that makes me so itchy.

Getting through the next handful of introductions and small talk with guests is exhausting. Way more exhausting than the first ones were.

And it's not just because of the elbow bump mishap, although that's part of it. I've heard that some people bump elbows instead of shaking hands, but I've never actually seen it happen before. How was I supposed to know that the awkward way the guy held his arm meant he was trying to elbow-bump me? And how could I have guessed that someone had turned in my direction with their drink so close to me, yet completely out of my line of sight, when I went in for a (in hindsight, too enthusiastic) elbow bump? So now I have to feel bad about the carpet, too.

And my feeling exhausted is not just because my compliment to a woman backfired, although that's certainly part of it, too. If I'd stopped to think for two seconds about the type of people I'm currently occupying a room with, I'd have known better than to burst out with, "I love your shoes! I have some in blue. Did you get yours at Target, too?" So I also add feeling bad for being the cause of the hurt look that crosses the woman's face.

It's also because I unknowingly offend someone's grandma. (May she rest in peace.) And because I make a comment about preferring one product over another, only to find out that I'm speaking to the head of product development for the company that makes the product I don't like.

Although the heels I'm wearing are not from Target and are to die for, I really am not looking to put my foot in my mouth again. Before I even have a chance to, Jaclyn steps up to me, linking her arm in mine, and says to Jackson, "Do you mind if I steal her away from you for a moment?"

She heads toward the kitchen, and without meaning to, I let out a massively relieved breath.

Jaclyn chuckles and leads us behind the long island counter. "I find the need to get away from the crowd now and then, too. I figured you might want to help me refresh the cheese tray."

"That's twice you've saved me tonight."

"Well, this is twice that you've dated my son and given

him a glow that only exists when you are in his life, so it only seems fair."

From where we stand, I can see across the dining room and into the room with all the people. Jackson is talking to a couple. His eyes shift just enough to meet mine, and he winks. That tiny little motion by him makes butterflies and hope spread throughout me. How can I like this man so much yet be so wary of the world that surrounds him?

I glance at Jaclyn as we work side by side, putting cheese slices and cubes on the tray. "Is this the house you moved to back when we were in high school?"

Jaclyn shakes her head. "This same city, but no. It was several miles away. Did Jackson ever tell you what happened?"

"He didn't." I am so curious to hear the answer now that it's unfathomable I haven't thought to ask the question before.

"I don't know if you remember, but when Jackson was a junior, our company started making a lot of money. I don't know why, but for some reason, we thought that meant we had to buy an expensive house in an expensive neighborhood. Maybe we thought our kids needed to start associating with other wealthy kids or to be in wealthier schools. I don't know. Why we ever thought that was a good idea for our kids at that point in their lives is beyond me. Maybe we just got too wrapped up in everything."

My eyes find Jackson, Naomi, Emma, Ethan, and then Jackson's dad in the crowd, watching them as Jaclyn talks.

"I'm sure you saw some of it before we moved. In fact, I'm guessing that's why you broke up with Jackson.

Anyway, it got a lot worse for all four of them once we moved. And it kept getting worse. We absolutely loved our new home. But one night, close to a year after we moved, Grant and I were sitting up in bed after everyone was asleep, and we came to the realization that if we stayed there, we would be ruining our kids. And we were willing to do whatever it took to save them.

"So that summer, we canceled the trip to Rome we had planned and instead took all the kids to Guatemala for six weeks to build homes in poor villages. They resisted the trip so much that we knew it must be the right decision. And it was. Living among some truly impoverished people changed us all."

That was the trip Jackson mentioned as his favorite. I find him in the crowd and can see the difference it made in him. Then I turn back to Jaclyn. "You were able to leave your business for that long?"

"That was very tough for Grant and me, for sure. Our company had been on quite the upward trajectory at that point, and there was the fear that if we took that break, we'd lose all momentum and the company wouldn't recover. But I think we needed that experience away from it as much as the kids needed the experience they got.

"We also decided that our kids' experience in Guatemala and the changes it made in them would just be forgotten if we didn't also get away from the situation that had caused it. So, we went to the people who we'd sold our home in Forest Grove to and offered to buy it back for a sizeable amount over what they had paid us for it.

"They jumped at the offer, so we moved back home just

in time for Naomi to start her senior year and the twins to start their junior year. Jackson went away to college, so we didn't get him back home until that next summer. It took a lot of work—much more than simply moving back into our old house—but I think we managed to undo the damage. We didn't move here until they were all graduated and off to college."

I look at Jackson and his siblings, then again at his dad. "It sounds like you and Grant made quite the sacrifice for your kids."

Jaclyn lifts a shoulder as she arranges the cheese. "'Sacrifice' means giving up something good for something even better, right?" She looks out at her family. "And raising kids who grow to be wonderful adults who we love spending time with is definitely something better."

I smile. "I think you did a good job." I pause a moment, and then a realization dawns on me. "That's why Jackson eats cereal for breakfast while watching cartoons even still."

Jaclyn's perfect eyebrows draw together. "Cereal and cartoons?"

Maybe she doesn't know. I like that it's something Jackson has shared with me.

His dad walks over to us and asks if Jaclyn would like him to take the tray to the party.

"No, I've got it." She picks up the tray. "You take a moment to escape."

Grant smiles at me. "I take it you're escaping, too?"

I nod, and he chuckles. "It can be a lot, can't it?"

We stand in silence for a few moments, Grant on one side of the island and me on the other, both enjoying the get-together from a distance. Then, Grant says, "Jackson tells me that you are designing costumes for a couple of plays at the Williams Theater. How is that going?"

I've forgotten how much Jackson's dad cared about what was going on in my life. He always made me wish I'd had a dad myself.

Work has been so far from my mind all night that his question jolts me back to it. "Really well. We've got a bigger budget for the materials than I usually have, and we've been able to do some really cool things with it. I can't wait to see my designs in action."

Jackson looks like he's ending a conversation with a trio of people and meets my eyes, a smile tugging at his lips. He starts making his way to me, walking with a grace that I now realize he gets from his mom.

"Did Jackson tell you that our family donates heavily to the theaters at Hamilton Hall? So, I've gotten to know a few of the directors."

My eyebrows shoot up. "He hasn't." Long before we started dating again, I knew that his family donated to a lot of causes and charities. They have a lot of art hanging on the walls of their home; it makes sense that they would donate to the arts because it's obviously important to them.

Jackson walks around to my side of the counter and wraps his arm around me.

"I better be getting back," Jackson's dad says. "But, Timini, I'll have to introduce you to the directors you haven't met sometime and see if they might want to send some more work your way."

I feel Jackson tense beside me. But by the time I finish

thanking his dad for his offer, Jackson's posture has relaxed, and he meets my lips with his in a quick peck. "I have one more person I'd like you to meet. And then what do you say we get out of here?"

"I would have to say, Jackson Oliver, that you have brilliant ideas."

CHAPTER 16

Jackson

I PULL into the gravel driveway of the house that Timini grew up in. Except for the tree out front that looks twice as big, the house is surprisingly similar to what I remember. Small, with reddish-orange brick, sparse grass in the yard, flowerbeds that are mostly weeds or dirt but always have a flower or two that seem determined to stand proud regardless of what any of their flower buddies want to do, and several wind chimes hanging around the house, their music tinkling in the slight breeze.

Timini told me that we didn't need to leave so early to come here today and that it was okay to be a little late. I pushed her to leave on time, though—I want to make a good impression. I grab the flowers I got for her mom, then get out of the car and go around to Timini's side to open her door.

I was excited to reintroduce Timini to my family. It took a lot longer for Timini to want to bring me to meet her mom again. I don't know if it's because she doesn't want our relationship to move to that level or if it's because she doesn't think her mom will be happy to see me again after all these years. As she steps out of the car, I decide to ask, even though I'm not sure I'll like either answer.

"Do you think your mom won't approve of me?"

Her eyebrows fly up and her head twitches back in surprise. "What? Why would you think she wouldn't? I don't know if you've had very many past girlfriends who've introduced you to their parents, but you're pretty much a parent's dream." She tips her head toward the flowers I hold. "Those are just frosting on the cake. She's going to love you."

I have to admit, that makes my chest puff out a little. But it doesn't help my confusion as we walk up the sidewalk toward the front door. "Then why were you so hesitant to bring me here?"

She shrugs as we go up the stairs to the porch and then she turns toward me as she pulls open the screen door. "You didn't exactly think my family situation was something to be proud of in high school. Things aren't much different now, so…"

My mouth falls open. Back when we were in high school, I didn't come to her house much—we mostly hung out at my place. Was that why? Did I really make her feel like her family or her home was something to be ashamed of? Sometimes I really wish I could have a talk with my high school self. "Timini, I—"

I'm cut off by her mom opening the front door, even though we haven't knocked or rung a doorbell. She must've heard us pull into the driveway. "Oh, goodness. You two are exactly on time. I wasn't expecting you to be here yet. Come in, come in."

Timini's mom isn't a single hair taller than Timini. Unless you count her actual hair—it's about the color of Timini's except for a few streaks of gray, but it's teased enough that it gives her a couple of inches over her daughter. Her face is bright and welcoming, and even though it's a dozen years older than the last time I saw her, it's obvious who Timini got her looks and her ever-present smile from.

"Mom, I'm sure you remember Jackson Oliver. Jackson, this is my mom, Flora."

I shake her hand, thank her for having us over, and present her with the flowers. She beams down at them. I look around at the living room that I haven't seen in so long. It holds a lot of stuff for such a small space, but it isn't messy.

"I am thrilled to have you and Minnie here," she says over her shoulder as we follow her into the kitchen. "Dinner isn't ready yet, of course, but maybe it will be by the time Keala and my grandkids get here."

A marinara sauce simmers on the stove, and Timini and I cut up vegetables for a green salad and chat with her mom while she prepares garlic bread. The kitchen is small and the table pushed against the wall is much too big for the space, but Timini seems so relaxed here. Until each time she meets my eyes. When she does, I can tell that she is suddenly seeing the space through my eyes and is worried about what I think of it. I make sure to keep my expression non-judgmental in any way.

Flora is just putting the garlic bread into the oven to broil when the front door opens and a mass of kids spill inside, an explosion of sound spilling in with them. The oldest looks about seven or eight and the youngest is a toddler. Then a woman hurries in behind them that I'm pretty sure is Timini's sister, Keala. If I remember correctly, she is about three years older and had already moved out when I started dating Timini in high school.

All the kids race to Timini or their grandma, and Timini scoops them into hugs as they come to her. Then she picks up the toddler girl and holds her on her hip. The sight strikes me in a way I haven't expected—there's a warmth in my chest but also a buzzing. I can't spend time trying to figure out what the emotion is because I want to take in Timini with her niece. There's something about her that just causes a…yearning. That's it. Huh.

Timini gives her sister a hug as the other four kids run around the legs of everyone in the cramped kitchen, and then she turns to me. "I don't know if you two remember each other, but Keala, this is Jackson, and Jackson, my sister, Keala."

Keala shakes my hand. "Of course! I totally remember you. You're the one who tore out Timini's heart, threw it on the ground, and then tap danced on it."

I grimace and scratch the back of my neck. "Yeah, I'm that one."

"Keala!" Flora says.

Keala gives me a big smile. "I'm the big sister—it's my job to give you a hard time. For what it's worth, I've heard nothing but good stuff about you lately."

Timini blushes and I have a hard time hiding a smile.

We all start sniffing the air at the same time, and a second later, Flora shouts, "The bread!" She grabs an oven mitt, and when she opens the oven door, thick smoke rolls out of it. A moment later, the high-pitched deafening beep of the smoke detector sounds.

"That means dinner's ready," the oldest boy calls out. All the kids laugh like this might be a joke they tell often.

To the sounds of four adults and five kids coughing in between laughing, Flora tosses me a hand towel and says, "Alarm's in the hall. Timini, grab that door."

Timini opens the door to the patio just off the kitchen, and Flora takes the sheet of garlic bread outside as I head to the hall and hold the towel like it's a flag I'm waving, trying to clear the smoke away from the alarm. I grin the whole time, remembering that Timini's dating profile said something about her needing a guy who wouldn't judge her by her inability to make food that wasn't supposed to be blackened. Apparently, it isn't just height and looks that she got from her mom.

Keala opens a window in the living room and turns on a box fan that is nearby, maybe kept there for this very purpose, and the smoke clears. Before long, we're pulling the table away from the wall, dishing up the food, and all crowding around the kitchen table. The ends of the table have chairs, but the two long sides have benches, which makes the squishing together easier. I somehow end up across the table from Timini, with her four-year-old niece and six-year-old nephew sharing a bench with me.

The pasta and marinara are actually quite good, so she

can cook just fine when she isn't distracted by a handful of kids. The conversation around the table moves quickly, gets interrupted frequently, and is often several conversations at the same time. Although there's so much going on with the kids that I'm not sure most of it can count as conversation.

Then the six-year-old boy on the other side of the little girl next to me turns and says, "Do you like kids?"

I smile and distinctly hear Timini stop talking in the middle of a sentence to hear my answer. "I do. I hope to have my own someday."

"How about today?" The boy pushes on his sister, sliding her down the bench closer to me. "Because we have an extra one. It'll only cost you five bucks."

The little girl turns to her brother and returns his shove. "I told you I can't be bought, so quit trying to sell me to random people!" Then she turns back to me, and in a much calmer voice, says, "But if you want to give me presents or candy, that would be okay."

I chuckle right along with Timini and her sister, but her mom gives a loud laugh that's contagious enough that all the kids start laughing, too.

When it dies down, Timini looks at her mom, studying her. "You seem so calm and happy today, Mom. Are you…" She looks around the room like she's noticing something for the first time. "Wait. Where's Neal? Why isn't he here?"

"Well," Flora says, straightening out her crumpled paper napkin and then folding it, "after the two of you came and helped me clean out the storage room, I just kept thinking how nice it felt to have all that old, worthless stuff out of the house and how great it was to free up so much space. It made me want to get rid of other dead weight, which got me thinking about other projects I wanted to take on. I realized that the dead weight I wanted to get rid of most was Neal. So I broke up with him."

"Finally!" Timini shouts and then reaches toward the end of the table to give her sister a high five.

The kids all pump fists and shout, "Yes!"

All I can do is look around the room at everyone's reactions, tilting my head to the side as I try to figure out why everyone is reacting the way they are to their mom and grandma breaking up with...her boyfriend, I guess, since none of the kids seem to view him as a grandparent. Still, it's kind of disturbing.

"You didn't like Neal?" Flora seems just as confused as I am, at least. So I'm not crazy.

"I just..." Timini seems to be choosing her words carefully. "...didn't like how much he made you constantly worry that no one cared about you anymore."

"You're supposed to tell me when a guy is no good for me!"

"Tell you?" Keala asks. "When you were as stressed out as you were with Neal living here? You wanted us to add to that?"

Flora draws in a deep breath and then blows it out slowly. "You're right. I probably couldn't have handled it. Although I did figure this one out and got him to leave on my own."

"And we are proud of you," Timini says, beaming at her mom.

We stay and play games with her family (including one

that seems to be called "All the kids huddle together to come up with a plan to tackle and then wrestle Jackson to the ground"). And even though we've been here for another couple of hours, the moment they all cheered to find out that Flora broke up with her boyfriend keeps unsettling me.

It takes half the car ride home before I figure out how to bring it up in a nonchalant way. Finally, I settle on, "I remember from high school that you said your mom went through boyfriends pretty frequently. I was surprised to see that she was still living in the same house. She never moved into a boyfriend's place?"

Timini shakes her head. "Nope. I think she knows not to do anything too permanent since none of her relationships last very long."

"She goes into them thinking they won't last?"

"No, she always expects them to last. Weirdly, she never sees it herself because I got to the point where I knew they wouldn't last by about the time I was seven. And trust me; it's a good thing that they don't last. She's never been the best judge of who will be a good fit with her."

Timini's life growing up was so different from mine. I can't fathom how it must've been for her to have never had a father figure in her home for very long. And if I'm being honest, it worries me a bit that Timini might not see a relationship as something that should last a lifetime. I want to straight-up ask her what her thoughts are on it but I can't right now. She's already been worried that I'll be a harsh judge of her family, and a question like that would only confirm it.

So, instead, I just ask questions I'm curious about. "Were

there any where your hope that things would work out overpowered your thinking that it wouldn't?"

At her silence, I glance over to see that she's biting her lip, thinking. "One, I guess. I was probably nine, and even I could tell that money was tight and that my mom was really worried that we'd lose the house. But she always said that we never had any reason to worry because things always worked out in the end. And then she started dating someone with a lot of money, and she thought—we all thought—that everything would work out. But that one *really* didn't."

I'm not going to ask any more questions about her mom. The answers are just filling me with dread. Instead, I switch the conversation to the charity dinner she'll be joining me for and Peyton's wedding that I'll be joining her for. If agreeing to attend two functions like that together isn't a sign that this relationship is serious, I don't know what is.

CHAPTER 17
Timini

OKAY, so admittedly, I have been dreading this charity dinner with Jackson. But now that I'm walking into the ballroom of the Sentinel, arm-in-arm with him, I realize that there are actually three really great things about it.

One, the event is mostly for business people, but it isn't like they're here to discuss business or how to be pretentious or anything like that. It's actually a charity dinner—the kind where people pay an obscene amount for a meal and all proceeds go to a charity.

That charity is the arts in the Portland metro area, which is cool. Because the more people donate to the arts, the more places like the theaters in Hamilton Hall can produce shows. And I've seen firsthand how much theater alone can bring up a community and the people in it.

Plus, the more they can produce shows, the more costume designers are needed. So events like this are helping me get that much closer to one day having my own space for my own shop. Then I'd be able to hire more people like Evie.

Two, I get to wear a fancy dress. This is one I designed myself months ago. Inspiration struck between projects, and I ran with it. I can't explain it, but with my height and build, wearing a full-length dress always makes me feel like a little kid. But this dress has the elegance of a long gown yet comes to just barely above my knees. The skirt is a little fuller but doesn't flow out like a princess's dress—it drapes beautifully, like a queen's. It's a deep purple and has a shimmer to it, and it makes me feel amazing.

Plus, my hair is up. Which means that it's easy to hide the lock that got burned off and still looks weird if I don't do my hair right.

And three, Jackson is wearing a tux. And oh boy, is the man on fire in a tux. He looks tall and lean, and his face is just so beautiful that I want to pull him into an alcove and make out with him for several long minutes. Or hours.

I must be sending those thoughts out there pretty loudly and Jackson must be catching them because he gives me a look that nearly turns my knees to jelly. Then he leans in close to my ear and breathes, "Have I mentioned how beautiful you are?" His breath is warm and tickles my ear, sending little zings of electricity down my neck and across my shoulders.

I turn to him, although I can't exactly get my lips as close to his ear even with these heels, and say, "Only a couple dozen times tonight. But don't worry—you aren't in danger of hitting the maximum number anytime soon."

He chuckles and then leads us along a pathway toward the table we've been assigned to but by way of a few dozen people who we stop to say hello to.

I can tell that this dinner is geared toward people who support the arts because of how beautifully decorated it is and how expensive the place settings look. Everything is in Kelly green and white, and the table centerpieces include the most unusual live plants I've ever seen. They look like a cross between a bonsai tree and a succulent.

Someone steps up to the podium on a stage at one end that I hadn't even noticed and asks everyone to find their seats so that dinner can begin. When I sit in my seat and Jackson tucks it in, I take a moment to run my hands over the soft fabric of the chair. Even it is elegant.

All of Jackson's family is present, but I'm dismayed to find out that none of them will be sharing a table with us. So that means our table includes six other people that I don't know.

The salad has the most vibrant, beautiful vegetables I've seen in a long time. The cherry tomatoes on it are especially huge. Like more-than-one-bite huge. I'm not about to bite into the tomato and have the insides squirt out onto the people sitting on either side of me. I cringe in embarrassment just thinking about it.

Instead, like a perfect lady, I decide to spear the tomato with my fork, gently slice it in half, and then eat half at a time. Except when I attempt to stab it, it instead flies from my plate to the middle of the table and lands on the bonsai-succulent like a too-big Christmas bulb.

My immediate instinct is to awkwardly stand, since my knees will have to stay bent—this tucked-in chair's legs aren't going anywhere on this carpet—and reach for it. Although, logically, I know that these tables are big and I can't reach it, I somehow still decide to try. Of course, the awkward standing just calls more attention to myself and what I've done. And it makes me come alarmingly close to knocking over the wine glass of the man to my left.

I sit back down, deciding that my tomato is just part of the centerpiece now, and glance at Jackson. He's just hiding a smile, gives me a wink, and leans in close to whisper, "I think it looks good there."

Okay, Timini, pull it together.

You'd think getting past the tomato-flinging incident would've calmed my nerves. Apparently, though, all the small talk is keeping my nerves on edge because those nerves, which have taken up residence in my hands, show themselves again not long after the wait staff serves the main course. In a move that I couldn't replicate if I tried, I pick up my fork and it flies out of my hand and lands somewhere under the table by my feet.

I make a move to reach for it, but Jackson puts a hand on my arm, stopping me. Instead, he looks over to the nearest waiter and holds up a finger. Within seconds, the man is at his side, and Jackson asks if he can bring a new fork. Yeah, in hindsight, that really is a better option than what had been my plan.

I swear I can act normal in social situations. Why does everything go wrong when I'm around people who care even more than usual that I act normal?

The waiter nods but instead of stepping away from the table, he bends down close enough to whisper in my ear. "Ma'am, you might want to check the back of your dress. It seems it got caught in one of the rungs of the chair."

My eyes grow wide and I suck in a breath as my hand flies to my backside. Sure enough, the skirt is elegantly draped upward, very un-queenlike, resting on one of the four rungs of the chair, lifting it enough that I'm sure I'm giving the tables behind me a perfect peek at my underwear in the space between the bottom rung and the seat.

My face burns red hot as I smooth down the fabric and tuck it under me as it should be. I dare a quick peek behind me to see just how many people might likely have caught the view, and several immediately drop their smiles and light chuckles right along with their gaze.

My mind scrambles back through the dinner, trying to figure out how and when I managed to get my skirt up there. Probably when I reached forward to grab the tomato, which still sits in its place of honor on the plant. How did I not notice it, though? Probably because the fabric of the seat doesn't feel so different from the fabric of my dress.

Moments later, the waiter places a fork next to my plate and gives me a small nod.

The dinner and the speeches can't end fast enough. It says volumes about my flubs since first sitting at this table that I am looking more forward to the "gather in clusters and socialize" portion of the evening than to the "eat delicious food" portion.

I briefly think of my mom and how she never seems to know when she is dating a guy who is completely wrong for her. She just seems blind to all the clues. And then, for a moment, I wonder if maybe my clues are all the things that are going wrong that don't usually go wrong for me.

No. I stop myself. I am *not* going to think that way.

We make our way to several groups of people that we hadn't said hello to on the way in and are currently standing with two couples and a single guy who are giving me looks like they definitely think I don't belong here. Okay, so I might agree with them, but they don't have to try so hard to make sure I am even more uncomfortable about it. Then, someone walks up to Jackson and says, "Can I pull you away for two minutes?"

The man doesn't need to apologize—I want to thank him for getting me away from this group! But then Jackson turns to me, gives my hand a squeeze, and says, "I'll be right back."

Oh. I'm not going with him. I'm staying with this group. I try not to panic and really wish I had Googled how to be better at small talk before I left home. Maybe I should just excuse myself to go to the restroom and Google it while I'm there.

I am opening my mouth to do just that when someone steps into the space where Jackson had been. I glance over to see it's Harper. The guy from the reception at Jackson's parents' home who Jackson really doesn't like. The one who had used him. Harper shakes everyone's hands, going around the circle, shaking mine last.

"It's good to see you again, Timini." He clasps his second hand on the outside, trapping my hand between his, his brows drawn down in concern. "I know how uncomfortable it can feel to be a fish out of water." He sucks in air through his teeth, grimacing. "I mean, you didn't grow up with any of this, right? It can be a lot to get used to. You have to deal with so many obstacles—everything from slippery silverware to wardrobe malfunctions. Tough stuff. Anyway, I've got to get back to Robin, but I wish you all the best in surviving the night."

I'm so in shock from his words that I don't even have time to form a thought before he walks away, leaving me with a burning face and a spinning head. I would escape straight to the restroom without even excusing myself from the other five people in this group, except that my eyes are still on Harper when he walks right over to where Jackson is talking with the man who pulled him away.

Harper's back is to me, so I can't see his facial expression, but he only has time to say a sentence or two before Jackson's eyes flash to mine, and they don't look happy. Almost accusatory.

I am still reeling from Harper's words and Jackson's expression when Jackson comes back over to join me. He doesn't slip an arm around my waist like I expect him to or ask if I'm okay. He just stands next to me, arms folded, like he is coming back to fill his hole in the group but isn't happy about it.

The other five have apparently switched the conversation from where Harper left it to education quite seamlessly because they've gotten pretty deep into the discussion while I haven't been paying attention.

"I mean, really, a Master's degree is the new Bachelor's," one of the men is saying, "and for most people, that isn't enough. If you only have a Bachelor's nowadays, you're no one."

The more he talks, the more I seethe. I am here to support Jackson, so I need to get out of here before I say some things that would be very unprofessional.

"And if you don't have a Bachelor's?" the single guy asks.

"Well, that's why they have jobs like flipping burgers and cleaning out sewage systems, am I right?" He claps a hand on the other guy's shoulder and they both guffaw.

I can't believe that Jackson is staying quiet through this.

The men haven't even finished laughing before the woman who is with the first guy turns to me and says, "Where did you graduate from, dear?"

I look at Jackson for a long moment, giving him plenty of time to say something before turning back to the woman. My pulse is racing, and heat rushes through me. I take a calming breath and then say, "I didn't. Now, if you'll please excuse me."

I walk out of the ballroom as fast as my five-foot-one height plus four-inch heels can take me. So, Jackson can manage to not let money turn him into a jerk when it's just the two of us, but he can't when he's around groups of people with money. And dinners like this are a big part of his life.

Which means that I can't be part of his.

"Timini, wait." I hear Jackson's footsteps behind me as I near the doors leading outside.

I turn to face him.

"I—" He starts like maybe an apology is coming, but it doesn't come.

I give him a small moment, and then say, "So much for your promise." Then I walk out of the hotel, already bringing up the app to request an Uber.

CHAPTER 18

Jackson

I SIT with my laptop in an empty conference room, trying to get through my emails. Not that I have to be in the conference room for this, but I haven't been able to focus at all in my office.

So far, the conference room isn't working, either.

I spot movement from the corner of my eye and glance at the door in time to see my entire family filing into the room. Naomi and my parents take seats around the conference table, Emma stays standing, and Ethan half-stands and half-sits on the conference table, all of them facing me.

"What the h—" Ethan glances at Mom. "Sorry, Mom. What in the world happened last night? The one time I saw you after the dinner finished was when you were by the wall, talking to Mitch. Then I saw Harper go over to you for, like, two seconds. I was wondering what he possibly could have to say to you and was on my way over to tell him to leave when you walked over to Timini. You were there for under a minute before she was fleeing toward the door like she never wanted to see you again."

My eyes drop to the table. "That's a fair assessment. I'm sure she doesn't."

"So what happened?" Ethan asks, spreading his arms wide.

"What happened was, I turned into an idiot." I run my hands through my hair, frustrated. "Just being around Harper always makes me question everyone's motives and wonder if people are getting close to me because of who I actually am or because of something stupid like money or influence or something.

"Timini was talking with the Chesworths and Finn McKee. After Harper joined them, he came over to me and said, 'Just a bit of friendly advice: you might want to keep a close eye on your girl. She found out how influential the people she was talking to are in the theater world, and she's name-dropping you like crazy to get what she wants.' And then I glanced at Timini, and she had this look on her face like she was appalled that he told me."

Emma had been pacing while I talked, but she stops and turns to me. "And you believed him?! *Harper*. The least trustworthy person you know. And you were like 'Oh, tell me anything about Timini and it doesn't matter how much I actually know her and you don't, I'll believe you.'"

Also a fair assessment. I can't believe my own stupidity.

Naomi shakes her head. "Harper probably has some plan. Like 'warning' you will get him back in your good graces so he can use you again. Or maybe he's just being petty. Why would you ever listen to him?"

"I don't know! Things have just been messing with my head lately. Like at that reception at our house—Dad, you and Timini were talking in the kitchen, and I came over just in time to hear you tell Timini that you were going to introduce her to people at Hamilton Hall."

Dad gives me a stern look. "She wasn't the one who brought it up. *I* did, because I know how serious you are about her, so of course, I would offer to do something that helps her."

I probably knew that. Of course, that is something Dad would do. And if I wasn't sure, I should've just asked him instead of letting it seep into my head like poison. No, I realize. I shouldn't have asked Dad. I should've just trusted Timini from the start.

"And now I've ruined everything. She broke up with me a dozen years ago because I was a jerk. I somehow got her to forgive me and trust that I am a different person now. And then I went and repeated history all over again. I was a jerk again last night, so she's got no reason to trust me."

Mom reaches across the table, squeezes my hand, and speaks for the first time. "You don't know that. Don't give up so easily, and don't take away her chance to choose that herself. But right now, go home, dear. It's clear just by looking at you that you didn't get any sleep last night. Sleep first, and then you'll be able to get things figured out when you wake."

I shake my head. "No, because then it'll be all I can think about. I need to be here so I can keep my mind busy."

Ethan leans forward so he can peek at my computer screen. "How's that working out for you?"

I let out a humorless chuckle. "Maybe not so well."

"I agree with your mom," my dad says. "You were supposed to be driving to the coast for Timini's roommate's wedding today, so no one was planning on you being here. You don't have any meetings. Go home."

———

I do go home, but I don't go to sleep. Instead, I flop down on my couch with the curtains open, facing the city but not really seeing it. Then I pull out my phone and open Chat Match for the first time since Timini and I switched to texting after meeting in person.

Then I start scrolling through our conversations from the beginning. It makes me long for her so deeply that it hurts.

It's strange reading everything now, knowing that it was Timini I was chatting with. And especially after getting to know her so much better over the last couple of months. Some parts make me laugh all over again. Some parts make me miss her even more. And some parts remind me of things I've already forgotten.

I get to the part where I asked what her biggest regret was, and I feel a physical pain in my heart when I read her words about not finishing college.

> Timini: It's whenever the subject comes up in conversation that I most regret it. Not being able to say that I graduated makes me feel inconsequential. Not capable of finishing things. Like I wasn't smart enough to do it. I avoid the conversation at all costs because it always makes me feel like a loser.

And then I feel a second stab when I read my own words, not too much further down in the conversation.

> Jackson: So I made a promise to myself from that point on to always step in and defend someone whenever they needed me to.

I didn't step in to defend her last night when she needed me to. Especially when it was regarding something painful to her. I've broken a promise to myself, and I've broken an unspoken promise to Timini. She knows it, too. I hadn't understood what she'd been referring to when she said, "So much for your promise" right before she left the hotel. But now I know for certain that she was talking about that promise.

I lie down on the couch, grab one of the couch pillows, and bury my head under it.

CHAPTER 19
Timini

IT IS EASIER to keep my mind off Jackson now that we are in the bride's room at the cute little reception area on the coast, helping Peyton get ready for her big day, than it was during our caravan from Quicksand to the coast. At least in this room, it is just the girls—me and my roommates. No couples.

Peyton is just so beautiful and so happy and so excited to become Peyton Peyton. Now that she has her wedding dress on—a fitted white one that flares just past her hips and is so very Peyton it should be named after her—we all stand around her, making sure her hair and makeup and veil and shoes and dress look perfect. Peyton is practically glowing, and the three of us are just basking in it.

"I can't believe the day is finally here," Peyton says.

Bex nods. "This was a long time coming. Emphasis on the 'long.'"

Peyton playfully smacks Bex's arm with the back of her

hand. "Hey, now. Not all of us can figure things out as quickly as you did."

"Well," Addison says, "I think it's sweet that you're marrying your best friend. I bet it'll be nice to have that friendship foundation in your marriage."

I reach out and twist a curl of Peyton's that isn't exactly right. "That, and the fact that you two are perfect for each other."

"We are, aren't we?" She gives a happy sigh, smooths down the front of her dress, and then turns toward us to wrap us all in a hug. "And I'm so glad that you are all here with me."

There's a knock on the door, and then Peyton's dad pokes his head in. "Hi, Sugar Bear. It looks like they're ready for us. Are you ready?"

"I am so ready!"

As the rest of us file out of the room, Peyton slips on her white, sparkly sandals and then hooks her arm in her dad's. The two of them are so sweet together. I try not to let thoughts enter my mind about how, if I ever get married, I won't have a dad to walk me down the aisle.

I follow Bex and Addison out to the beach where everything is set up for the ceremony. Just behind the minister stands a simple arch with gauzy sea foam green fabric draped along it. A carpet of the same color leads from the edge of the wooden patio down the center aisle to where Max stands in a light gray tux, looking like he is as happy standing in the sand as he would be standing on a cloud in heaven.

Which is practically the case—the waves coming into the

shore in the background, the ocean sounds, the shades of blues and greens that are only found on the shore, the sandy beach—all of it is pretty heavenly.

Two rows of four seats sit on either side of the carpet, keeping things small and intimate, just like Peyton wanted, and I know almost all of the people sitting in them. Ian and Roman are already seated on the front row on the left-hand side, with empty seats next to them for Addison and Bex. Max's friends Hunter, Emilio, and Leo—the three we all went camping with back when Max was trying to convince Peyton that they should be more than friends—are all seated on one side along with Hunter's wife and Emilio's and Leo's dates. Max's mom sits on that side, too, with an empty seat beside her that is probably for Peyton's dad.

On the row behind my roommates are the grandmas next door, Shirley, Carol, and Meera. Which leaves one seat next to them for me. As I slide into my seat, it strikes me how badly I wanted Jackson sitting here, an empty seat beside him, waiting for me. And how badly I miss him.

No matter what, though, I am going to keep my emotions in check. This is Peyton's day.

Meera leans over Carol to give me a fist bump and whispers, "Welcome to the single ladies' row!"

This is the first of my roommates' weddings where I hadn't needed to go find someone to be my date for the evening. It's the first one where I had a date set up and assured for weeks. It is also the first one I've shown up to without a date at all.

Carol leans toward me and says, "I always wanted a beach wedding."

"Oh, yeah?"

Carol nods. "I mean, who wouldn't? This is gorgeous!"

"I wouldn't." Usually, I never think about my own wedding or if it will ever happen. I find myself actually thinking about it, now, though. "When I get married, it isn't going to be someplace where I can't wear heels."

Carol chuckles and pats my knee. "Your time will come. And when it does, you wear the most fabulous heels you can find."

The soft music coming from the speakers changes to the wedding march and we all turn in our seats. Peyton and her dad are nearing the end of the wooden patio. Her dad looks like he's going to burst some buttons on that tux shirt with how proud he is, and Peyton looks like the universe has come together to turn this one moment in time into perfection, and she's wearing a smile to match.

I turn to see Max's reaction just as he brushes under his eye with his knuckle. As long as he waited for Peyton to view him as more than a friend, I can see why getting to this moment would bring a tear.

We all swivel in our seats as Peyton and her dad walk up the aisle. Then he gives her a kiss on the cheek, squeezes both her hands, and takes his seat next to Max's mom.

Back when I first signed up for Chat Match, I had zero plans of finding someone to have a serious relationship with and definitely wasn't looking for a future husband. But seeing how happy and in love Peyton and Max are as they hold hands and smile at each other while the minister speaks, and seeing my blissfully wedded roommates sitting on the row in front of me makes me actually yearn for it.

And it makes me miss Jackson horribly. Most of my dating experiences with guys have only lasted one or two or three dates. I have had a few relationships that have lasted over a month, though. Each time I ended things with one of them, I actually felt a huge sense of relief. Ending things with Jackson brought me no relief—only heartache as I've never known before.

Peyton and Max have written their own vows, and as they recite them, almost everyone is reaching a knuckle up to dry a tear.

Once they finish promising to always be there for each other, the minister pronounces them husband and wife. They kiss the sweetest kiss, and cheers erupt from all of us before they break the kiss and turn to us, grinning. Peyton motions to have all sixteen of us come in for a group hug. Then she goes around and gives us all hugs individually.

When Peyton gets to me, she holds out her bouquet. "This is for you."

My eyebrows draw together. "What? Why?"

"You know—the bride tosses the flowers to the single ladies and one of them catches it. But I wanted to give it straight to you since you're the only one of us still single."

"I am not the only single lady! There's Shirley, Carol, and Meera. And Max's mom. They're all single."

Shirley places a wrinkled hand on my arm. "But we've all been married before."

I motion to where Emilio and Leo stand with their dates. "And there are two more single ladies over there." I hold my hands out like a shield between the flowers and me. "Really, you should toss it. It's tradition, and I know how much you want a traditional wedding."

"Are you sure?"

I nod with complete conviction. "Yes. Please." That bouquet represents hope, and hope is dangerous. Sure, I ache for Jackson. But something has changed for him, and I'm not sure he still feels the same way.

Peyton nods once. "Okay. I'll toss it." She gathers the three grandmas from next door, Emilio's and Leo's dates, and even manages to get Max's mom to join in.

But I don't stand with the others. Instead, I take a seat in one of the vacated chairs to watch. Peyton turns her back to the group and then tosses the bouquet high into the air. And I guess she doesn't know her own strength because it goes sailing over the heads of all of the single ladies gathered to catch it.

But to everyone's delight (based on how much they are cheering), Carol, Meera, and Shirley are the ones who go running for it. Then, in a move that surprises everyone, Meera leaps for it. She jumps high enough, but instead of her hand grabbing onto the bouquet, she just bats it, sending it hurling at a much faster speed straight at me. I don't even have time to fully get my arms up to protect myself before the bouquet smacks me right on the forehead.

And then it falls into my arms that were going up to protect my head.

Honestly, I didn't know that seventeen people could cheer so loudly. I let out a breath of a chuckle at the absurdity of it all. Then, as I gaze at the flowers in my hands, the full force of how much I want a life with Jackson—dinner parties and business receptions and all—comes crashing down on me. The emotions that I have been working so hard to keep inside all day long spill out and run down my cheeks.

Within seconds, Peyton, Bex, and Addison are wrapping me in a group hug. A second or two after that, Shirley, Carol, and Meera add themselves to the hug.

They hold me for a long moment as silent tears run down my face. Then Peyton, who is the closest to me, tips my chin up, brushes away my tears with her fingers, and tucks some of my hair that has fallen into my face (including the short piece that was burned) behind my ear. "Things will work out," she says in a voice that is so sure and so confident that I believe her. "You will get everything you never knew you wanted—because you never did make that list of what you wanted in a man—and you will get your happily ever after."

"You will," Bex says. "And then we'll have a group date where we eat amazing food, watch *Flip My House, Not My Life*, give unsolicited advice, and have a dance party with all of us."

I hug all the wonderful ladies in my life and let myself hope that they might be right.

CHAPTER 20

Jackson

I WAKE up from a very rough night at the sound of my doorbell. I'm still in the same spot on the couch where I crashed last night, still in yesterday's clothes. All I managed to do was eventually close the curtains. I ignore the bell.

Then I hear a weird knocking on the door like it's from an elbow instead of knuckles.

"It's Naomi. Let me in, Jackson."

My head throbs. Whether it's from dehydration or from the terrible nightmares I had all night, it's hard to tell. "Go away."

"Remember how you let the front desk know that I could have a key to your apartment so I could come in and water your plants when you were on long trips? I'm betting you never revoked that. Don't make me go all the way back down to get a key from them. Because I will, but I will drop the açaí bowl I brought you in the trash on the way down if you don't let me in. And it has all your favorite toppings. Even dragon fruit."

I sigh and get up. If my sister is one thing, it's persistent, so there's no sense fighting it. Of all the people I might have expected to show up on my doorstep, though, I would've guessed Emma, not Naomi. I open the door, and Naomi comes in, a container in each of her hands.

"Thanks for not making me go back down. I wasn't about to toss the bowl I brought for me even if I did toss yours, and I planned to eat it in front of you and make you totally jealous." She sets them down on the bar counter, motions to one of the bar stools, and says, "Sit." Then she goes around to the kitchen side and gets out two spoons before making a detour to the living room, grabbing the remote, and pressing to open the curtains covering the floor-to-ceiling windows.

Sunlight spills into my apartment as she comes back to the bar and hands me a spoon. "Dude." She wrinkles her nose as she takes in my disheveled state. "Don't you have a morning routine that you never stray from? You should've stuck with it today."

I'm not sure I want to do anything today. "Is that why you came over? To tell me to shower, shave, and put on clean clothes?"

She takes a bite of her açaí bowl. It looks good, but I'm not sure my stomach can handle eating mine.

"I hadn't planned on that. But now that you mention it, let's add it to the list. No, I came over to get you out of your funk and kick you into action."

I just look at Naomi, not quite understanding what she

means. It's Saturday. It's not like she needs to get me off to work or anything.

Naomi lets out a long sigh and then sets her spoon down, turning to face me. "I want Timini as a sister-in-law. So I'm here to help you figure out how to win her back."

My head jerks up in surprise.

"I like her. And I think you really do, too."

I nod.

"Do you love her?"

I loved her a lot back in high school. Enough that it took a very long time to get over her and move on. It really didn't take long into our relationship this time around before I fell for her just as deeply. And I've been falling even more in love with her daily since then. "Yeah, I do."

Naomi nods like I'm confirming what she already knows, and then picks up her spoon and takes a bite of her fruit. "She's the most down-to-earth person I know, and I know that's important to you. She's also fun and kind, and I've actually seen some of her work as I've helped out with the arts side of our charity. She's pretty incredible."

She is. All of it.

"I wish you could see yourself from our point of view. Ever since you started dating Timini again, you've been happier. Calmer. More…self-assured. Confident. Focused. Hopeful. You come up with more creative solutions to issues at work. And, to the shock of everyone, you've been more flexible. You no longer stress so much about little things not going according to your schedule."

A few of those things I have noticed in myself. Most I

hadn't before Naomi pointed them out. All I know is that I'm happy and I like who I am when I'm dating Timini.

"But most of all, I've seen the way she looks at you. She loves you, Jackson. You. Not your job, not your money, not your influence. *You.* And as a sister, I can't see my brother get someone like that in his life and then stand by and let him just mess it up. This needs fixing."

I realize that both times I dated Timini, she always liked me for me. The outside things that people in my circles always seem to like me for are actually repellents to Timini. She doesn't like fancy dinners or networking events, yet she still goes to support me.

She has looked beyond all the biggest, loudest, most obvious things in my life and saw through to the core of who I am. It is a gift I haven't experienced in my life for a long time.

"*How*, though? I'm not sure it is fixable. I put her in a situation I knew she was uncomfortable with. I'd been trying to get a quick meeting with Mitch for weeks, and I knew he wouldn't talk about his company possibly helping ours with this Delhi thing if Timini was present.

"But I never should've left her in the presence of three people I knew were arrogant, pompous jerks. Well, four, once Harper showed up. But then, when I came back, I just stood there while they attacked, knowing that they were attacking her Achilles heel."

My stomach roils just thinking about it again. How could I have done that?

Naomi smacks my shoulder with the back of her hand.

"Honestly, I sometimes wonder how we can even be siblings." She stares at her açaí bowl for a long time and then pushes it away. "Well, I think you need to prove to her that you can be trusted. And however you do it, make it meaningful."

I nod.

"And then don't *ever* be someone she can't trust again."

I let out a humorless breath of a laugh. This is one lesson that is burned so deeply into me that I don't think I'll have to learn it twice.

"Ever."

"I know."

"I'm serious, Jackson. You've got to have her back, always. No matter what."

"I promise," I say with a more firm conviction than I've ever made a promise before.

"Okay," Naomi says. "Go shower. Take longer than seven minutes, and while you're in there, figure out how you're going to win her back."

CHAPTER 21

Timini

AFTER WE ALL make the drive back to Quicksand the day after Peyton's wedding and Peyton and Max head off on their honeymoon, I go straight to my room and think about unpacking the overnight bag I took. Then I decide I don't care and just drop it on the floor by my closet.

I turn around to see Bex and Addison at my door, a bowl of peanut M&M's in Addison's hands.

"Can we come in?" Bex asks.

"If you're bringing peanut M&M's, then always."

The three of us sit on my bed in a circle, the bowl of candy in the middle of us. Rain is pouring down outside, so it's dark and gloomy, just like I'm feeling. But it also makes me think of how Jackson actually likes being in the rain, which makes me miss him even more.

Bex told me a few weeks ago that I self-sabotage relationships. I was defensive about it at the time, but I spent the whole drive home from the coast thinking about it. "Do you guys know why I self-sabotage?"

"Timini," Addison says, "I don't think that what happened was your fault—"

"No. I don't need you to…" I let out a frustrated breath, not knowing how to explain. "Listen. This is important. I need to figure it out."

Addison nods. "Okay, then, we'll help you. Uh, I'm guessing it probably has something to do with your mom and how her boyfriends are always bad for her."

"I know that I grew up thinking that things were always worse when you were with a guy, and I kind of internalized that. It was probably the reason why I always chose to date the kind of guys I did because then I knew I wouldn't be with them for long." I shake my head. "But I don't think that's my issue with Jackson. I just don't know what is."

"Oh," Bex says. "I've got an idea. Addison and I will list, rapid-fire, every reason we can think of that might be the issue, based on what we know of your situation growing up. When one hits you differently, stop us."

"Okay." I sit up straighter, ready to figure this out. I try to get in tune with whatever part of me is at my core so I will recognize when one of the things they say is it. The thing I need to know. "Let's do this."

"Guys don't stick around for long," Bex says.

No.

"Love isn't worth the struggle it causes," Addison says.

No.

"Guys don't make you a better person."

No. Jackson totally makes me a better person.

"You aren't attracted to the right guys."

No, because I am attracted to Jackson, and he feels like the right guy.

"Love doesn't last."

Nothing. This isn't heading in the right direction.

"You don't believe relationships can work."

"It's easier to quit than work things out."

"You don't need a guy in your life."

"No," I burst out, frustrated that none of it was right. "It's because my dad left, so I'm afraid to give my heart to a guy." I gasp, my eyes wide as my hands fly over my mouth. I stare in shock at my friends for a long moment as my own words sink in. "It's because of *my dad*? I did not know that!"

Bex and Addison both reach out a hand and hold mine as I work through things out loud. "I didn't know my dad. He was like all of my mom's other boyfriends—there for a bit and then gone. I wasn't born yet when he left. I don't even remember wondering about him much as a kid—I haven't thought about him in ages."

My brow crinkles. "That's really my issue? I didn't know my dad had ever had a part of my heart—let alone that it made me afraid to give it to anyone else for fear they would leave like he did." Somehow, knowing that makes it easier. It makes me realize how illogical it is. And that means I have the ability to set my mind and emotions straight about it.

"Remember when you were setting up your profile for Chat Match," Bex says, "and you told us you didn't know what you wanted in a guy? Maybe that was the reason why you never stopped to figure it out. You were afraid of a relationship getting to the point where it would matter." I'm quiet for a long moment before I say, "I did figure out what I want in a guy, though."

"You did?" Addison asks. "When?"

"When I was sixteen. I'd just forgotten that I had. Before I found out that Jackson was Jack, I had a dream that I was on a date with Jack and we kissed. Oh, stop giving me those looks. Anyway, when I woke up, I thought back to the date I'd dreamed about that Jack and I actually had. We'd been stargazing after an amazing date, and at that moment, I knew I wanted a guy who would care for me and love me just like Jack did. I wanted a life like the one I'd experienced with him that evening." I take a long, slow breath and then bite my lip. "Do you think I overreacted at that charity dinner?"

Bex looks thoughtful. "I've been to a lot of events like that. Most of the people there are great. There are always a few who are exactly like the ones you experienced that night. I wish I could've gone to that one! I would've stuck by your side the whole time and kept all the awful ones away. Knowing what those kinds of people can be like, do I think you overreacted by leaving that night? No, I don't."

I look down.

"Do I think you overreacted about Jackson's part in it? I don't know. Tell us about the other times Jackson has been a jerk."

"Like back when we were in high school?"

"No," Bex says. "From dating him now."

I blink as I scour my memory. "Just that one time."

"Do you think there was something more going on that night?" Addison asks.

"Harper, this guy who already burned Jackson a while ago, did go over and say something to him."

"Any guesses what he said?"

I shake my head. "Right before going to Jackson, Harper was telling me how I wasn't nearly good enough to be there. If he'd gone over and said anything like that to Jackson, though, Jackson probably would've punched him and then come to my rescue."

And I suddenly know to my core that's the kind of man Jackson is. The kind who would come to my rescue, not the kind who would stand by while people poked at my insecurities. I don't know why he did something so out of character that night, but I know that's not who he is. I want to give him a chance to explain.

And I desperately want a chance to fully move past all my own relationship fears and have the life with Jackson that I knew I wanted clear back when I was sixteen.

CHAPTER 22

Jackson

I ALWAYS MARVEL when I'm thinking about someone and then I get a text or an email or a phone call from that person soon after. I've been thinking about Timini nonstop for quite a while now, so maybe it's not the same thing, but I'm about to send her a text to see if we can talk when one comes in from her.

Timini: I miss you. Do you think we can get together and talk?

Relief whooshes out of me. She's willing. And she misses me. I just stare at the text for a moment, letting the hope it contains wash over me. Then I respond. I want to type yes in all caps, with several exclamation points. And maybe add the heart balloon expanding. But I hold back.

Jackson: I miss you, too. Any chance you could meet me here tonight at 7:00 at Mocha Falls? It's an outdoor café by my building.

I feel bad asking her to come to me—I should be moving heaven and earth to get to her. But I can't actually move my building, and it's kind of key to my plan. Well, it is if things go okay at Mocha Falls.

———

At ten minutes to seven, I'm sitting with two dark mochas at a small outdoor table right next to an eight-foot-high water feature that mimics Proxy Falls. When I chose a seat, I thought that maybe the water cascading down over moss-covered rocks would calm my nerves, but I still have twitchy muscles and a rolling feeling in my stomach. Hopefully, though, the falls will make Timini smile.

From knowing her, I doubt I'll see her until about seven-fifteen, so I tell my bouncing leg to calm down. But it's barely seven-oh-one when I see her rounding the corner to the open café. She's wearing those jeans and heels again that I love, along with a jacket, which I'm glad about. The night is warm currently, but I'm not sure it will stay that way.

And she's wearing a smile. It's a nervous smile, full of trepidation, but a smile nonetheless. There's not a lot in this world I wouldn't do to see that smile.

I stand and wave, and her eyes immediately fly to me as she walks over.

She glances at the waterfall next to our table, and her

mouth twitches like she's fighting a smile. "I see you took my offer to heart to join me when you changed your mind about bodies of water."

I had hoped her mind would immediately go to our conversation through the app about bodies of water and how she prefers them to water falling from the sky. We both sit down, and I say, "Well, I'm not afraid to admit when I'm wrong."

I hadn't even planned to say that and didn't mean for it to be a segue into what I want to say. Maybe it just came out because it's been on my mind so much.

"I talked to Roman," I say, and her eyes flash to mine. "I hope that was okay. He told me what happened with the Chesworths and Finn McKee. But mostly about what Harper said to you while I was gone."

Hearing from Roman what Harper had said to Timini makes my heart ache for her. "I am so sorry I left you open to that. I wish I never would've gone to talk to Mitch."

She nods but stays quiet.

"But that doesn't explain my part that night. Not that it excuses what I did at all. After Harper poked at your fears and doubts, he came over and poked at mine, too." I let out a humorless laugh. "And, obviously, you handled it about a million times better than I did. I reacted by being the worst kind of jerk at that party. You deserve to have someone who has your back no matter what. Someone who will stand up for you in any situation." I pause for a moment and then add, "And I want to be that guy."

She studies me, and I hold my breath, waiting for her

response as a slight breeze blows past us, bringing the scent of coffee from the outdoor café.

Finally, she nods and smiles. "I really want you to, too." Then she reaches forward and takes my hand in hers.

I look down at our hands, marveling at her. "Based on your background and all you've been through, I am baffled at how forgiving you are. I think you might be the most forgiving person I have ever met."

Timini shakes her head. "I'm not, though. I don't do it often. I think that *with my background*, I've learned to really trust my gut and to act based on that. When it comes to forgiveness, well, that's when I've learned to trust it the most. My gut seems to like you." She smiles. "And your family."

I swallow hard, as the understanding of what a gift she's giving me fully hits me. "I want to be the one person in your life who doesn't need your forgiveness. I can't promise I'll never stumble, but that's what I will always be striving for."

Her eyes go back and forth, scanning mine for a long moment. Then she stands, grabs hold of the fabric of both sides of my jacket, and pulls me to my feet. Then she tugs me to her and presses her lips against mine. Her kiss is soft yet fierce, and through it, I can feel that she's missed me and has worried that she was losing me every bit as fully and achingly as I have worried I was losing her.

I wind my fingers in her hair, holding her close, and her grip on my jacket tightens. My body seems to melt, and I move my hands to the sides of her neck and slide them to her shoulders. Then I pull back from the kiss just enough to whisper against her lips, "So, does this mean you want to stay together?"

"Yes, it does."

I smile against her lips and then whisper, "Will you come with me? I want to show you something."

In answer, she tucks her hand into mine, and I lead the way to my building.

CHAPTER 23
Timini

I WALK WITH JACKSON, tucking myself into his side and reveling in how great it feels to be with him again as he leads me around the corner to his building.

When I left that charity dinner without Jackson, I thought it was because I couldn't trust him. I studied him intensely as he apologized, and I was blown away by how much I knew, deep in my gut, that I trust him. Probably more than I trust anyone. People make mistakes. I do all the time. Pretty much daily. I can forgive Jackson for making a mistake, especially when he fully owns it and has such a desire to not make the same mistake again. I want him to do the same for me.

And at the top of the list of things I know that I can trust without a doubt is this man's love for me. And mine for him. Even when we were teenagers and had so little experience with relationships, I knew what we had was something special. I'm not saying that we didn't both need to go off and figure ourselves out, but I am very glad that we found our way back to each other after all this time.

And this time, I think we truly understand exactly what we have.

As we walk past the front desk attendant in his building's lobby, the man smiles at us and winks. Then Jackson leads me to the elevator bank. I know that he lives on the twenty-first floor, so I'm surprised when he presses the option for the roof and then slides an access card into the scanner. I give him a questioning look, but he just looks at the digital sign above the doors that shows which floor we're on.

That's okay. I can be patient and wait to see why we're going to the roof.

Or maybe not. Patience isn't exactly my strong suit.

To keep from asking, I focus on the screen that shows the floor numbers we're passing and counting how many ones I see as we ascend. Thirteen of them. That's a lot of ones—that has to be a good sign. And in between glancing at the floor indicator, I distract myself by noticing how amazing Jackson looks in that casual button-down, those jeans, and that jacket. He is just so very handsome.

The elevator doors open to a roof that is very different from the one I've been picturing. Instead of being covered with gravel, it's tiled with big slate tiles. Glass goes up from the edge all the way around, forming a safety barrier between the roof and the ground below, and, I realize, making it look from the ground like the roof area is just another floor. And everything is so clean.

A man wearing a hotel uniform stands ten feet in front of

us. When we step off the elevator, he smiles at the two of us, then says to Jackson, "Everything is ready for you."

Jackson thanks the man and shakes his hand, doing the sneakiest job I've ever seen of passing along a tip. The guy gives a curt nod and then also gives Jackson a wink before stepping into the elevator.

Once the doors close, we're alone on the roof. It's a rare cloudless night, and the moon and a few of the brightest stars shine above us.

"What do you think?" Jackson asks, and I manage to pull my gaze away from the beautiful man in front of me to look out over the city.

The view is incredible. All the lights from a city with over half a million residents shine around us in every direction. It's breathtaking.

He grabs hold of both of my hands and says, "I read back through our messages in Chat Match from the beginning, back before I knew you were you and you knew I was me. And I realized that when we were both talking about our favorite dates, we were talking about the same date. The one we went on at the end of your sophomore and my junior year. Since it was a date we both loved, I thought maybe we could do something similar tonight. With a few modifications."

My pulse races, and there's a lightness in my chest that makes me feel like I'm floating. Although part of that could come from being on, essentially, the twenty-ninth floor.

He reaches his hands up to my shoulders and turns me in a direction I haven't looked yet. A blanket is spread out on the tile, a picnic basket on it, and a tall lamp spills golden light down onto the blanket. A large outdoor movie screen is set up, too, along with a projector. Jackson walks over to the blanket as he talks. "The 'day date' part of that date we had for the dance—the photo scavenger hunt—didn't really fit into the plan, especially since it isn't exactly 'day' right now. So that means dinner is first."

He sits down on the blanket, and I sit beside him. It's fluffier than I expected. He must've put some kind of padding under the blanket to make the tile floor feel more like soft grass.

"When I asked you in a message what your favorite foods were," he says, pulling container after container from the basket, "you mentioned quite a few."

"Oh my goodness," I say, putting a hand over my mouth. "Did you really get them all?"

Jackson grins. "I've got Mexican, Thai, Chinese, pizza, Italian, and"—he pulls one last container out of the basket—"cheesecake."

"*Without* almond extract?" I ask.

He chuckles. "I even double-checked. And don't worry— I didn't get full meals at any one place."

We each eat a taco from Taco Sabroso, some red curry, an egg roll, a mini pizza, and some ravioli. And in between them all, bites of cheesecake.

"So," Jackson says as he finishes a bite of curry, "if the combination of a carnitas taco, an al pastor taco, and a fish taco give superpowers, do you think a carnitas taco combined with this many types of food will grant us anything?"

I savor a bite of cheesecake as I consider the combo. Then

I nod. "It'll definitely grant us a superpower. Possibly accidental time travel. Or we might start glowing."

"Or the ability to speak squirrel."

"Or to find the perfect parking spot anywhere in Portland. Or maybe levitation."

"So, what you're saying is, if my feet leave the ground, I shouldn't panic."

I smile. "That's not from the food. The feeling of soaring is just from being with me."

Jackson laughs, and I soak in the joyful sound. It's just so good to talk with him. To be near him. To spend time with him. To eat a meal with him. To know that there will be more of this in my future.

Just like the date we went on in high school, we go to "the dance" after dinner. Instead of being in the high school gym, though, it's on a rooftop overlooking the Portland skyline. And, just like at our high school dance, we dance to *All of Me* by John Legend, *A Thousand Years* by Christina Perri, and *I Won't Give Up* by Jason Mraz.

For each of the three songs, I relish being in Jackson's arms as we dance even more than we did back in high school. He's different now. I'm different. Both things make our relationship even better. Stronger. I look up at him. "Please tell me we will do this often."

"Every night, if you'd like."

Once the third song ends, Jackson pulls back a bit. The grin on his face is so wide it makes me smile, too.

"Okay, during that date, the movie was next. You told me once that you loved Hallmark movies, so I did a lot of

Googling to find the one that people liked more than any other. I figure that we could watch that one."

"Be still my heart," I say, putting a hand over my heart. "Did I really find a man who will watch Hallmark movies with me?"

"You did. But, I propose we do things out of order tonight and go straight to stargazing first." He takes my hand and leads me to the glass wall that surrounds the roof. "You might have noticed, though, that, unobstructed view or not, downtown Portland isn't exactly the best place to stargaze. So we are going to have to light gaze instead."

The glass wall rises almost to my shoulders, and I rest my elbows on the top of it, looking out over the lights of the city. It really is incredibly beautiful and mesmerizing.

After several minutes of "light gazing," Jackson turns toward me, a more serious expression on his face. "Timini, I really want you in my life."

"Oh, thank heavens. Because this was going to get awkward really quickly if you didn't."

Jackson chuckles. "I promise to be *by* your side and to always be *on* your side. Even still, I know that if you are in my life, it would often put you in an environment that you wouldn't necessarily appreciate. Would you be okay with that?"

"Well, you've seen the state of the round tables in the dining room at the inn. I figure if you are in my life, you will just as often be subjected to environments you don't necessarily appreciate, either. If you can handle it, I can, too."

He brushes his knuckles along my jawline, sending

shivers across my neck and back. "You are one incredible human, you know that?"

"I'm pretty sure that's why you love me." It's a bold response, but I'm feeling bold tonight.

"That, and a lot of other reasons."

"Oh, yeah? Tell me more about these reasons."

"I am pretty sure I love everything about you. Your kindness. Your willingness to try new things. Your strength. Your creativity. Your ability to find a solution to anything. Your ability to not feel guilty about being late."

I playfully smack him on the arm. He chuckles and says, "The way you keep me from sticking so strictly to a schedule and being inflexible. I love that you stay up late, that your preferred outside temperature resembles an oven, and that you see the beauty in a messy bed."

"You do not love those things about me."

"Oh, now, see? That's where you're wrong. I love them all because they're all part of you. And I love all of you."

"Okay. Then I'll say that I love your morning routine. That you eat cereal and watch cartoons, wake up early, like the freezing rain, look out for others, look out for me, volunteer so much, and are pretty much to die for in a suit."

The corner of his mouth twitches up in a smile.

"Oh, and I can't forget your ears. You do actually have really great ears."

He laughs a loud, happy laugh.

"Which is great, because here I thought it was just one of those things a guy would say in a dating profile that wasn't true. So I'm feeling pretty lucky that it turned out to be one hundred percent real."

He gives me a look then, so pure and genuine and sweet, and I want to put my hands on his face just to feel it, too. But before I get the chance, he drops to one knee, and my hands fly to my mouth.

"Timini. I want nothing more than to have you in my life always. Please say you'll marry me, and I'll promise to always have your back, no matter what, in everything that you do. And I'll make sure your car always has gas in it. And I'll bring you cookies from that restaurant on Belmont every time you're doing bills or business accounting. And I'll bring you the magical trio of tacos from Taco Sabroso every time you have a deadline. And I'll love you more every day forever and ever, and I'll never stop doing everything I can to show that to you."

I'm laughing and crying so much I can barely breathe or see. I wipe the tears from my eyes, then pull Jackson to standing, take his face in my hands, and kiss him. "Yes," I say, and kiss him again. "Yes, I will." I kiss him again. "Of course, I will marry you." I kiss him some more. "Yes, yes, yes."

And then I give up talking and kiss him until I'm breathless.

Epilogue

MEERA

I **HOLD** Bex's phone up to where it shows my face at a flattering angle instead of at the double-chin angle that so many people my age use, and then I press the record button. Then I say, "Hello, Bexlandians! I don't know about you, but I am thrilled that Bex let me take over the camera to film a Hidden Inn Roomies Segment for her show and to give you one final update. I am here with my own roomies, Shirley and Carol."

Shirley and Carol both crowd into the frame and wave.

"These two oldie-locks and I have been friends longer than most of you whipper-snappers have even been alive. But I'm here to update you about Addison, Bex, Peyton, and Timini, not us."

"No," Carol says, "you've got to press that button to flip the screen."

"Oh, get your hands off. I know which thing to press." I tap the correct button, and the screen shows everything else, so the three of us make our way through the maze of boxes in the kitchen where Addison, Bex, Peyton, and Timini are all talking as they stand at the kitchen island, eating veggies and dip. "This room is feeling so vacant and echo-y right now. And can you even believe it took this many boxes to pack up this room? Actually, I think it was even more because some have been hauled out already.

"Anyway, the update! Let's start with Timini because tomorrow is her big day! Yep, folks, you heard it right—the last of these gals to break the 'No falling in love' pact they all made when they first moved in is getting married tomorrow!"

Addison, Bex, and Peyton all cheer and scream, and Timini smiles widely.

"Look at her face glow. I hope you can see it through the camera. Tell us all about it, Timini."

Timini sighs. "Jackson is just the most amazing guy ever. And we're getting married! I still can't believe it's true. And oh my goodness, y'all, he is tears-in-your-eyes beautiful in a suit. And tomorrow he'll be in *a tux*. Which I know will bring tears to everyone's eyes. I'm sorry you can't all be there to witness it. You'll just have to take my word for it that there will not be a dry eye in the place just from looking at him."

I flip the camera so it's back on me. "I am going to second that statement. Not that I've seen Jackson in a tux. Or a suit, really. But I've seen him in a dress shirt and slacks and I had to pretend that I got dust in my eye. Tell us about the wedding." I flip the camera back to Timini.

"Okay," Timini says. "Well, Jackson and I grew up in

very different worlds. I mean, we went to the same high school and all, but still very different. Our engagement was probably twice as long as my family thought it should be, but only about half as long as his family thought it should be. In the end, we chose the date that was how long *we* thought it should be.

"Well, actually, I would've married him soon after he proposed, so I guess the date we chose was kind of a compromise, too. Which is what marriage is all about, right? So it seemed fitting. And because we've only been engaged for four months, it limited where we could have it, which actually worked out well, because it meant we couldn't have it at any pretentious venues. I mean, don't get me wrong, the place is still crazy nice and all the guests are going to love it. And Jackson and I do, too. But it won't be an uncomfortably nice place, you know?"

"And where are the two of you going to live?" I ask. You know, I really should be a professional interviewer. I'll have to ask Bex if I can get into something like that at age seventy-two.

Timini's smile widens. "At his apartment in downtown Portland. Mostly because it's so very pretty! I mean, it comes in second to the man himself, but it's nice. And it has floor-to-ceiling windows overlooking Portland. Plus, it's where he's lived while we've been falling in love, so…" Timini lifts a shoulder in a shrug, her cheeks reddening. It's so cute, and I'm pretty sure the viewers at home will be able to see that just fine.

"And after the wedding tomorrow, they're going to soar off to their honeymoon! In Italy, right?"

Timini grins. "I've always wanted to go there."

"Okay, Bex! You're up. Bex and Roman have been living here while their house was being built, and it took quite a bit longer than they thought it would, didn't it?"

"If you've watched my other videos, then you've probably heard some of the story. Basically, everything went wrong every step of the way, but now everything is right. It's just three months later than we thought it would be. But the house is perfect. So perfect. We had the final walk-through and closed on it just a little over a week ago. Roman and I have both had crazy busy work weeks, so we've just been moving things over slowly. The day after Timini's wedding, though, we plan to move everything else in and then happy dance for a good week straight."

I turn to Peyton. "Peyton, your home-buying experience hasn't quite been the same, has it?"

Peyton giggles. "No, thank the stars. We found the cutest little house ever! And I'm not even joking, it has a white picket fence out front. It's right here in Quicksand, and the backyard butts up to the woods. So someday when we have little kids, Max will practically be able to take them camping in our own backyard. And the inside of the house is adorable."

"And when did you close on the house?" I already know the answer, but I think Bex's listeners might get a kick out of Peyton's answer.

"Six weeks ago. We tried to have the closing day later, but the people selling it had to move for work and couldn't wait any longer."

"But you haven't moved in yet?"

Peyton shakes her head. "Why in the world would we move when everyone else is still living here? We didn't want to miss out on this kind of fun!"

I chuckle and aim the camera at Shirley, who is just shaking her head.

"Okay, Addison. You're up. So, you've got your three best friends and their husbands—or in Timini's case, very soon-to-be husband—moving out within the next few days. What are your plans?" I am so excited just asking the question that I can barely get it all out.

"Well," Addison says, "Ian owns the house next door."

I turn the camera back to myself. "That would be the house that me, Shirley, and Carol live in, for those of you following along at home." Then I switch it back to Addison.

"Ian and I decided that we would like to start a family in the next year or so, so we chose to move into his house."

I switch the camera back to myself. "And that means that the oldie-locks are moving into Hidden Inn!"

I press the phone into Bex's hands, and Bex aims the camera at me, Shirley, and Carol as we dance like music is playing and everyone is watching. Which is pretty much the same as dancing like no one is watching only with more gusto. We dance in place and move and jive and even do a TikTok dance that my granddaughter taught me once.

"Did you hear that, folks?" Carol says. "It's going to be out with the new and in with the old!"

"What do you think, ladies?" I say to Carol and Shirley. "Should we make our own pact to not fall in love, just like these ladies did? You saw what it did for them."

Shirley does a dance move that looks like she's stomping

on invisible bugs. "I say we do it! I'm single and ready to get nervous around anyone I find attractive."

I nod. "Aren't we all. Addison, there's one thing you and Ian are going to need to know before we become neighbors again by switching homes. You're going to be hearing a lot of loud music at all times of the night because we are going to be partying it up over here!"

Carol nods. "Very loud music. Our hearing isn't what it used to be, you know."

Bex laughs loudly and turns the camera back on herself. "And there's your update, Bexlandians! Wish the soon-to-be new residents of Hidden Inn the best of luck in the comments. While you're at it, you might want to wish Addison and Ian the best of luck living next to such noisy neighbors. And give the biggest congratulations to Timini and Jackson! Remember to like this video and tap the subscribe button. Until next time, goodbye from all of us!" She pans the camera around to all of us and then shuts it off.

"Aww, you guys," Timini says. "I can't believe this is our last night with all of us together!"

"Don't," Peyton says. "You're going to make me cry again."

Addison motions for her roommates to come in for a hug. "I just want to soak in every last minute we have together." She wraps her arms around Timini, Peyton, and Bex. "There are great things on the horizon for all of us, and being here together made so much of it happen. I love you, ladies."

There is a chorus of "Aww, I love you, too!" coming from all of them.

"Make room," Carol says. "We want in on this hug."

I squish in with my roomies, and I wrap my arms around everyone I can reach in our seven-person hug and squeeze tightly. It isn't going to be the same without them all living here. Which, as far as I'm concerned, means that we are going to have to have game nights frequently and invite them all.

"I think we need to do one last dance party," Timini says. "With music."

"On it," Bex says, tapping her phone.

Within moments, music sounds through the Inn's speakers, and all seven of us are dancing around the half-dozen round tables in the dining room, giving them a send-off to remember.

Author's Note:

I hope you enjoyed this final book in the *How to Not Fall* Series! If you have read all four books, you've read the epilogues for each of the four couples. Even after I finished writing this final epilogue, though, I still couldn't stop thinking about these characters and where their lives led them after Timini and Jackson's wedding. They are a hard group of people to let go of!

I decided to write a series epilogue that takes place one year after the series finishes, and Addison, Bex, Peyton, and Timini each get to narrate a chapter in this scene with all of them present. (With plenty of commentary from the grandmas next door!)

If you'd like to join my VIP newsletter subscribers, you can tap here to get the How to Not Fall Series Epilogue FREE.

—Meg

Get your copy

Romancing the Spy

WANT TO READ MORE OF MEG'S ROMANTIC COMEDIES?

Need more adventure and humor in your life?

In a family where the spy business is the family business, falling in love is the real mission impossible. Follow the six Lancaster siblings—each uniquely trained, fiercely loyal, and more than a bit protective—as they navigate top-secret missions, unexpected romance, laugh-out-loud situations, witty banter, an abundance of chemistry, and lots of adventure.

Spies Don't Fall for Their Asset

Spies Don't Fall for Their Rival

Spies Don't Fall for Their Neighbor

Meg Easton is the *USA Today* bestselling author of contemporary romances and romantic comedies with fun, memorable, swoon-worthy characters, and settings you'll want to pack up and move to. She lives at the foot of a mountain with her name on it (or at least one letter of her name) in Utah. She loves gardening, bike riding, baking, swimming before the sun rises, and spending time with her husband and three kids.

She can be found online at www.megeaston.com

Sign up to receive her newsletter and stay up to date with new releases, get exclusive bonus content, and more.

If you liked this book please leave a review. Your review can help other readers find books they might fall in love with.

youtube.com/@megeastonauthor

bookbub.com/authors/meg-easton

instagram.com/megeaston_author

facebook.com/MegEastonBooks

tiktok.com/@megeaston_author

www.ingramcontent.com/pod-product-compliance
Lightning Source LLC
Chambersburg PA
CBHW061818190726
48289CB00007B/2238